D0678706

DAWN AMBUSH

Fargo held a finger to his lips, then ducked back down.

She'd be no help to him. She was bound and gagged, seated on a hard chair in the center of the room. He didn't want to wake them up and put them on the alert, even though there was a chance one of them might come outside and make for easier pickings.

But Mrs. Madrid might get hurt in the process. Fargo didn't want that.

And so he silently made his way around the crude cabin, to the door. Carefully, he tried the latch.

But it was ajar, and the door softly creaked open at his touch.

He couldn't believe his luck.

But when he took one step inside, the floorboards gave him away. He froze at the painful creak. Early turned over, but didn't wake up. Fargo wasn't so lucky with Two-Bit.

Two-Bit's eyes popped open, and half a second later he pulled his gun. Fargo fired before he did, though.

And fired again at Roy Spriggs, who was by that time scrambling free of his blankets, gun in hand.

Mrs. Madrid screamed despite the gag in her mouth, as Fargo wheeled back to face Early Truffle. But Early's timing was off. He was just reaching for his holstered gun, hung on a peg on the wall, when Fargo cocked his gun again and said, "Not so fast, Early."

THE
TRAILSMAN
#268

New Mexico Nymph

by

Jon Sharpe

A SIGNET BOOK

SIGNET
Published by New American Library, a division of
Penguin Group (USA) Inc., 375 Hudson Street,
New York, New York 10014, U.S.A.
Penguin Books Ltd, 80 Strand,
London WC2R 0RL, England
Penguin Books Australia Ltd, 250 Camberwell Road,
Camberwell, Victoria 3124, Australia
Penguin Books Canada Ltd, 10 Alcorn Avenue,
Toronto, Ontario, Canada M4V 3B2
Penguin Books (N.Z.) Ltd, Cnr Rosedale and Airborne Roads,
Albany, Auckland 1310, New Zealand

Penguin Books Ltd, Registered Offices:
80 Strand, London WC2R 0RL, England

First published by Signet, an imprint of New American Library,
a division of Penguin Group (USA) Inc.

First Printing, February 2004
10 9 8 7 6 5 4 3 2 1

The first chapter of this book originally appeared in *California Casualties*, the
two hundred sixty-seventh volume in this series.

Copyright © Penguin Group (USA) Inc., 2004
All rights reserved

REGISTERED TRADEMARK—MARCA REGISTRADA

Printed in the United States of America

Without limiting the rights under copyright reserved above, no part of this
publication may be reproduced, stored in or introduced into a retrieval sys-
tem, or transmitted, in any form, or by any means (electronic, mechanical,
photocopying, recording, or otherwise), without the prior written permission
of both the copyright owner and the above publisher of this book.

PUBLISHER'S NOTE
This is a work of fiction. Names, characters, places, and incidents either are
the product of the author's imagination or are used fictitiously, and any resem-
blance to actual persons, living or dead, business establishments, events, or
locales is entirely coincidental.

BOOKS ARE AVAILABLE AT QUANTITY DISCOUNTS WHEN USED TO PROMOTE
PRODUCTS OR SERVICES. FOR INFORMATION PLEASE WRITE TO PREMIUM MAR-
KETING DIVISION, PENGUIN GROUP (USA) INC., 375 HUDSON STREET, NEW YORK,
NEW YORK 10014.

If you purchased this book without a cover you should be aware that this
book is stolen property. It was reported as "unsold and destroyed" to the
publisher and neither the author nor the publisher has received any payment
for this "stripped book."

The scanning, uploading and distribution of this book via the Internet or via
any other means without the permission of the publisher is illegal and punish-
able by law. Please purchase only authorized electronic editions, and do not
participate in or encourage electronic piracy of copyrighted materials. Your
support of the author's rights is appreciated.

The Trailsman

Beginnings . . . they bend the tree and they mark the man. Skye Fargo was born when he was eighteen. Terror was his midwife, vengeance his first cry. Killing spawned Skye Fargo, ruthless, cold-blooded murder. Out of the acrid smoke of gunpowder still hanging in the air, he rose, cried out a promise never forgotten.

The Trailsman they began to call him all across the West: searcher, scout, hunter, the man who could see where others only looked, his skills for hire but not his soul, the man who lived each day to the fullest, yet trailed each tomorrow. Skye Fargo, the Trailsman, the seeker who could take the wildness of a land and the wanting of a woman and make them his own.

New Mexico Territory, 1858—
The siren's song targets the strongest of men,
making the most beautiful of women
deadlier than a loaded six-shooter.

1

"Easy, boy, easy," Skye Fargo whispered to the Ovaro as he carefully rode down the steep trail behind Early Truffle's hideout.

Early and his boys had held up the stage from Lone Pine to Quake, New Mexico, a week before, and Fargo had been hired to go out and bring them in, along with their captive.

Well, not exactly hired. Pressed into it was more to the point.

Either way, here he was, in the New Mexico hills, tippy-toeing down a sharp, wooded slope, trying to sneak up on the gang.

It was early morning, barely dawn. Smoke rose in a thin plume from the cabin's chimney, likely smoke left over from last night's dying fire. Early, despite his name, didn't rise with the sun.

These boys had not only held up the stage, but they'd killed the driver and kidnapped young Mrs. Diego Madrid, the bride of Señor Diego Francisco Esteban Rodriguez Madrid, owner of the second-largest rancho in New Mexico, and a friend of Fargo's from way back.

Sort of. Fargo hadn't reminded Madrid that the last time they'd met, Madrid had lost fifty-seven dollars to Fargo and hadn't paid it. Of course, a little range war had broken out right in the middle of the card game, but Fargo really didn't think that was any excuse.

If Fargo came back with his wife—and the Los Galgos payroll that the stage had been carrying—Madrid might be a little more keen on remembering that small pot.

Or so Fargo hoped.

The Ovaro, a tall, gleaming, black and white stallion, made it down the slope without making a sound, and Fargo reined him to a halt while he was still back in the woods. Or at least, the low, spotty vegetation that passed for woods in these parts. He looped the horse's reins over a branch, then crept forward.

Scuttling to the cabin's side, he moved forward, along the outside wall, until he was just under the window. He took a careful peek inside.

It was just as he thought.

Early Truffle was asleep in his bunk. Two other men—Roy Spriggs and Two-Bit Thompson, Fargo thought—dozed in bedrolls on the floor. The only person awake was the extremely attractive Mrs. Madrid, whose brown Spanish eyes grew round as saucers when she turned her head and spied him.

Fargo held a finger to his lips, then ducked back down.

She'd be no help to him. She was bound and gagged, seated on a hard chair in the center of the room. He didn't want to wake the outlaws and put them on the alert, even though there was a chance one of them might come outside and make for easier pickings.

But Mrs. Madrid might get hurt in the process. Fargo didn't want that.

And so he silently made his way around the crude cabin, to the door. Carefully, he tried the latch.

It was ajar, and the door softly creaked open at his touch.

He couldn't believe his luck.

But when he took one step inside, the floorboards gave him away. He froze at the painful creak. Early turned over, but didn't wake up. Fargo wasn't so lucky with Two-Bit.

Two-Bit's eyes popped open, and half a second later he pulled his gun.

Fargo fired before he did, though.

He fired again at Roy Spriggs, who was by that time scrambling free of his blankets, gun in hand.

Mrs. Madrid screamed despite the gag in her mouth, as Fargo wheeled back to face Early Truffle. But Early's timing was off. He was just reaching for his holstered gun, hung on a peg on the wall, when Fargo cocked his gun again and said, "Not so fast, Early."

"Damn you, Trailsman!" Early snapped, although his voice was still a little groggy with sleep. "Where'd you come from, anyhow? How'd you get in on this deal?"

"Never you mind," Fargo said. "Now, suppose you busy yourself getting Mrs. Madrid untied." When Early, grumbling, moved to untie her, Fargo added, "There's a good feller, Early."

Free at last, Mrs. Madrid rushed into his arms, nearly knocking the gun from his hands. He managed to catch her and still keep it aimed at Early, though.

"Oh, thank you, thank you, sir!" she babbled. She turned out to be a staggering beauty underneath that gag, too. He had to keep on reminding himself that she was a missus, not a Miss, and that her husband was a friend of his. Sort of.

"The name's Fargo, ma'am," he said when she stopped for air. "Skye Fargo. Your husband sent me."

"Bless him! Bless you! Kill this last animal!"

She made a grab for his gun hand, as if she could force him to pull the trigger, but Fargo held her off.

"Hold on, lady," he said. "Your husband wants 'em in one piece." He looked over at the floor, where Two-Bit Thompson lay dead. Roy Spriggs wasn't doing much better. "Well, one'a them, at least," he added. He jerked the gun's barrel at Early. "Get your hands out in front of you, Early."

Mrs. Madrid set a fist on either hip. "Who is in charge now, Mr. Stage Robber?"

Early made a face.

Fargo handed Mrs. Madrid his spare pistol, telling her to aim it at Early and shoot if need be, and then he got busy with the rope.

"You say that perhaps we will reach town tomorrow?" Mrs. Madrid asked.

They had camped for the night. Early Truffle was hogtied over by the horses, and Fargo was just dishing up some grub.

"Yes," he said. "Tomorrow."

It wasn't soon enough if you asked him. Mrs. Madrid was a beauty, all right. Her looks, in fact, were nearly transcendental. Dark Spanish eyes, long lashes, the face of an angel, and the body to match.

But she had turned out to be a bitch of the first water. That afternoon, when Fargo had asked for her first name, she had snidely said, "You may call me Mrs. Madrid. Or Señora Madrid, if you are so inclined."

She'd said it in a way that made him feel like she was addressing a servant, not her savior.

It kind of pissed him off, to be truthful. He didn't remark on it, though. He just figured that he'd soon be shed of her, and he'd never have to see her again. So in the meantime, he only spoke when spoken to.

It was easier.

Except that as she took her plate she asked, "They have found my sister?"

Hell, he hadn't even known she had one. And if her sister was lost, why had she waited so long to ask, anyhow?

"You lose her?" Fargo asked, settling back with his supper. "Careless of you."

4

She didn't understand the dig. She just looked at him oddly, then said, "She lost herself. To the West. You do not know of this?"

Fargo bit a corner off a biscuit. Chewing, he shook his head.

"Well . . ." Mrs. Madrid said, and gave him a look that finished her sentence. The look said, *If you are not important enough to know, then perhaps I shouldn't have spoken.*

Fargo didn't press her on it. He was too hungry, and too annoyed with her already. He didn't need to be told once more that he was no better than a piece of shit under her shoe.

Especially by the stuck-up wife of a man who owed him fifty-seven dollars.

They pulled into Quake early the next afternoon. Fargo turned Early Truffle—and the payroll—over to the town sheriff, drew him a map of where he could find the hastily dug graves of Roy Spriggs, who had died, and of Two-Bit Thompson, who had died as well.

The sheriff thanked him politely, then locked up the money and threw the map away.

He also gave Fargo a voucher for three hundred dollars, which surprised Fargo to no end. "This for Early?" he asked. "Didn't think there could be more than fifty bucks on his head."

"Oh, he knocked over a tradin' post outside Santa Fe," the sheriff replied. "Shot the owner. These things add up, you know."

Fargo stuck the voucher in his pocket. "I guess they do," he said with a shrug.

And then he escorted Mrs. Diego Madrid up to the hotel, and her husband.

When he knocked at the door of the Madrids' suite, Madrid didn't answer it himself. Rather, a butler, classically English, did.

"Madam," he said, showing no emotion whatsoever.

5

He bowed just slightly. "Welcome home. I trust you are unharmed."

She didn't answer him, just walked on past. Fargo just stood there watching her go, and then realized the butler was still standing there, waiting.

"Testy, ain't she?" he asked.

"One would believe so, sir," said the butler. "Mr. Madrid would like to see you as well, at your convenience."

Fargo stepped through the door and took off his hat. "He'd better. The bastard owes me fifty-seven bucks from two years ago."

The butler, leading the way down the hall, said, "I'm terribly sorry, sir."

"Don't call me sir."

"Yes, sir."

Fargo gave up. He was also just beginning to realize that Madrid had the whole top floor of this building, not just a suite of rooms. He was impressed. The cow-ranching business must be profitable these days.

Just then, the butler stopped before a door and rapped softly.

"Enter!" shouted a voice—Madrid's.

Fargo expected to find him with his wife, but he was alone when the butler opened the door.

"You've found her?" Madrid asked, brightening when he saw that it was Fargo.

"She's around here somewhere," Fargo offered.

"Indeed, sir," said the butler. "Shall I—"

Madrid waved him into silence. "No, no, Foster. She will come when she is ready. She is bathing the trail dust away, no?" he asked Fargo, but didn't wait for a reply. He simply gestured the butler out, then gestured Fargo to one of two leather chairs beside the window.

"My friend," Madrid said, joining him in the opposite chair. He reached for the brandy. He said, "I am so pleased!" He paused. "She was unharmed?"

Fargo nodded. "None the worse for wear. And I'm

happy for you, Madrid," Fargo said, leaning back. It was a nice chair. "Be happier if you'd pay up on that gambling debt."

Madrid actually looked surprised. "I owe you money, Fargo? From when?"

"From a few years back," Fargo said. He took the small glass that Madrid offered and swirled the amber-colored liquid. "You remember when we were in that seven-card-stud game, and young Danny Florez came runnin' in smack in the middle of it and—"

Madrid smacked his forehead. "Ay! How careless! Fargo, please forgive me. I had forgotten completely. Here, let me make it right."

Madrid rose and crossed the room to his desk, and pulled out a black velvet pouch, then a fistful of coins. He returned to Fargo, who was still holding his untouched brandy, and he began counting out coins from those in his hand. "It was fifty-eight, was it not?"

"Fifty-seven."

"Honest to the last penny!" Madrid said with a grin. "A man can always count on you, Fargo. There," he said, placing the final coin in Fargo's hand. "Fifty-seven. And your reward for the return of my lovely Rosa." He plunked the velvet bag into Fargo's hand, too. "I cannot tell you what a happy man you make me."

Fargo sat there, staring at it. "You mean, there was a reward?" He meant that several ways.

"Yes, certainly!" Madrid sat down again, and he looked suddenly thunderstruck. "You mean to tell me that you have gone out on the trail of my wife and these miscreants with no thought of a reward? That you did it out of friendship and friendship alone?"

Actually, Fargo had done it just to get that fifty-seven dollars back, but he suspected now wasn't the time to mention it.

He shrugged.

"How did I come to deserve such a friend?" Diego

7

asked the ceiling, and ostensibly, someone far above it. He gripped Fargo's arm, slopping Fargo's brandy just a little.

"Don't go gettin' all choked up, Madrid," Fargo said, gently freeing his arm. Madrid always had been on the emotional side. It was that hot-blooded Spanish flair, Fargo guessed. He pocketed the coins and the little pouch, though, just in case Madrid changed his mind about the reward.

"You will stay to dine with us?" Madrid asked, and Fargo didn't have the heart to turn him down. "Yes," Madrid continued. "You will stay. And I think I will have another job for such a good friend. One I would only trust to you."

Fargo lifted his brandy and toasted Madrid, then drank. If it would pay—and right about now, Fargo was pretty damned sure that it would—he was all for it.

2

Madrid left Fargo to his own devices for a time—
ostensibly to see about his newly returned wife—and
Fargo made good use of the time. He wandered
through the public rooms of Madrid's home away
from home, checking over the paintings and the
furniture.

Now he knew why Madrid insisted on referring to
his wife as Mrs. Madrid instead of Señora Madrid.

Madrid had always been an Anglophile, but he
seemed to have gone crazy for it lately. The place was
full of English paintings: Gainsboroughs and Turners,
and a plethora of pre-Raphaelite painters like Edward
Burne-Jones, all new since Fargo's last visit to the
hotel, graced the walls. Of course, he hadn't been here
except once, five years ago, but it was still a great deal
of new art.

And all English.

The furniture was English, too. While the study had
been decorated mostly in an English country style, the
parlor was Georgian, and the dining room was Re-
gency, complete with an ormolu clock.

And of course, there was the butler.

There was even a music room—nothing in it except
a lacquered, and very English, grand piano and bench,
its closed top piled with stacks of sheet music. The

9

only other furnishing was a lone music stand, several feet away. The walls were hung, from floor to ceiling, with layer upon layer of thick and colorful tapestries, and the windows were cloaked with heavy drapes.

Odd, he thought. He knew Madrid didn't play—at least, he hadn't when Fargo had met him. He had a distinct memory of Madrid drunkenly trying to pick out "Mary Had a Little Lamb" on the old upright in a saloon, and of him failing miserably.

Maybe the wife was the musician in the family.

Old Madrid, Fargo thought sadly, had gone round the bend. Here he had the blood of Spanish kings running through his veins, and he wanted to trade it off for the rather cold and dreary background of England.

At least Spain was sunny. Not unlike the part of New Mexico where Fargo found himself today, and where Madrid had chosen to live. At least, part-time. He knew there was a large ranch—and a very grand hacienda—not a half day's ride from town.

But maybe he hadn't chosen, Fargo thought, correcting himself. Madrid had inherited this land from his daddy, and his daddy before him, and Lord knows how many daddies before that—since the 1500s, Madrid had once told him. And three hundred years was a very long time.

Fargo was jarred from his thoughts by footsteps, followed by the entrance of Mr. and Mrs. Madrid. She was smiling now, something she hadn't done once since he'd freed her. He hated to pay her the compliment, but it suited her. It certainly belied the darker side of her disposition.

"Fargo," announced Madrid jovially. By his tone and the look of his wife, Fargo could guess what they'd been doing while he was cooling his heels, taking in the artwork. Madrid said, "Come and eat with us, my friend! Foster has laid the meal."

*　　*　　*

"You want me to *what?*" Fargo asked. His fork was poised over his Yorkshire pudding, and he couldn't believe his ears.

"You act as if I am asking you to lasso the moon, compadre!" Madrid said with a laugh. "I am only asking you to find one small woman. You have already proven you can do that." He gave his wife's hand a squeeze. "And you will be paid handsomely, I promise you that!"

Now, Fargo had counted the money Madrid paid him while he was waiting for the happy couple to return, and so he had no doubt that Madrid's reward would, indeed, be handsome. But the job he'd have to do for it!

He shook his head. "I don't know, Madrid. See, I was thinkin' about going up north. Mayhap to Montana or the Dakotas, and I—"

Madrid waved a hand. "You can do that later, amigo. It is not pressing business, is it?"

When Fargo shrugged, Madrid announced, "It is settled, then. My darling, the great Skye Fargo will find your dear sister and return her to us."

"Excellent," said Madrid's wife. "I have been so worried! That's why I was coming home, you know. Because of my dear sister. Until those fiends took me for ransom." She scowled.

"Did I tell you?" Madrid asked. "My lovely Rosa is half English." He beamed proudly. "Her great, great, great aunt was in the court of King George."

"Well . . . good," Fargo finally said. It was the best he could come up with on short notice.

Even though his innards were in a knot over the prospect of this new assignment, he raised his glass in a toast.

"Pip-pip, cheerio," he said dryly. Then he added, beneath his breath, "and all that other shit," before he upended his glass and drained it.

* * *

"She is a lovely thing," Madrid was saying, over brandy and cigars in the study. His wife had retired for her afternoon siesta. Even the siren song of good, English breeding couldn't overcome some things, Fargo thought.

"Marga—that's her nickname, for Margarita," Madrid went on, "—is the baby of my dear Rosa's family. Their parents, they are dead."

Fargo nodded. Naturally, it would fall to Madrid to take care of his wife's siblings, then.

"But Marga," Madrid continued, "Marga is . . . different." He stopped, and seemed to be hunting for the right words. Fargo couldn't help him.

At last, Madrid appeared to give up looking for a polite way to say whatever it was that was worrying him. He took a deep breath and announced, "She has too much love for the men. There. I have said it. I'm afraid that she is a wanton, Fargo." He turned away, toward the window.

Little things like that had never bothered Fargo. In fact, he rather enjoyed them. Or, at least, enjoyed taking advantage of them. But he kept his face and tone serious, for Madrid's sake.

"She wasn't kidnapped, was she?" he asked.

Madrid shook his head. "No," he said, still looking away. "She ran off with some sort of salesman." Suddenly, he wheeled back to face Fargo. "A salesman! A common drummer, as you call them! If Rosa found out, she would be shamed forever."

"And you want her brought back," Fargo said. He took a sip of his brandy, then added, "What if she doesn't want to come back? What if she and the fella are happy? Hell, Madrid, what if they're married?"

But Madrid—a darkly handsome man who, when Fargo first ran into him, had been a gunfighter, struggling against his own tyrannical father's parental bonds—shook his head. For a moment, Fargo thought he was going to spit on the floor, but he didn't.

Madrid said, "No, Fargo. Not Marga."

"She's done this before?"

"Twice. And always the same. She runs away, runs out of money, and comes home." Madrid paused to relight his cigar, which had gone out.

"The first two times," he went on, "I have found her myself. But this time?" He shook his head. "I cannot go. I cannot leave my business concerns, or my beloved wife. And I confess, the life of a landlord has left me softer than I would wish. I can no longer ride the trails and sleep on the ground."

You don't want to, you mean, Fargo thought. But he didn't say it. Madrid had been a good friend to him, and there was no need to embarrass him now.

Instead, he said, "So you figure to send me, instead."

Madrid nodded, almost apologetically. "Yes. I do."

Fargo figured that his goose was as good as cooked, but he decided to just let nature take its course. Besides, he reasoned, what fellow wouldn't want the job of transporting a sex-crazed young gal cross-country? Some men would say that was a dream job.

Of course, in Fargo's case, it was likely to get bollixed up. That'd be just his luck.

But then, it might not . . .

"When'd she take off?" he asked.

"She disappeared last Tuesday," Madrid said. "More brandy?"

Fargo held his hand over his glass, thwarting Madrid's attempt to refill it. He figured he'd best have his senses about him.

Madrid shrugged. "Suit yourself. At any rate, she ran away with one Mister Cort Cleveland, a representative of the Bowling Green Glass Company. They manufacture lamp shades and doodads," he added with a trace of shame. "Or so I am told."

Madrid walked to the desk and opened a drawer. Pulling out a small silver picture frame, he handed it to Fargo. "This is Marga," he said.

Fargo turned the picture over in his hands. Suddenly, he was more than willing to take this job, because the girl in the picture was downright gorgeous! "Wow," he whispered under his breath.

But Madrid heard him. Or perhaps he just knew Fargo too well. "Yes, she is beautiful," he said. "Too beautiful for her own good."

Fargo was silent. He was still staring at that Spanish face with its startling light eyes and raven hair, which beckoned him to touch it. Her lips were full, sensual, and slightly pouting, her pale eyes—gray? blue? green?—gazed from the photograph, full of want and need, hungry for him.

Or perhaps she'd had a little fling with the photographer. Hard to tell.

He wrenched his gaze away.

"How old is she, anyway?" Fargo asked, and turned the picture over, face down, on the end table. "She looks young."

"Twenty-two," Madrid said. "She is getting old. Two times I have arranged a marriage for her, but she always does something, says something, to break it off."

Madrid slumped down into his chair, shaking his head. "You would think that a woman like our Marga, with her proclivities, would welcome marriage! It escapes me. Am I getting to be an old man, Fargo?"

"Hell, no," Fargo replied. "I never have understood the female sex worth a damn. Ain't got nothin' to do with age."

For instance, he didn't understand how Rosa, Madrid's wife, could be so goddamn standoffish when her sister was hugging the buttons off everybody within a ten-mile radius. At least, to hear Madrid tell it. He tried to think of an old quote he'd heard somewhere, something about opposites and bedfellows, but it escaped him for the moment.

"Which way did they take off?" he asked.

"West," Madrid said. He raised his brandy glass again and drained it all at once, probably in relief. "They took the stage that left three days before my Rosa was due back. It was on account of Marga's disappearance that Rosa cut her trip to the north short and returned home. Almost home, that is."

Fargo nodded. She was coming home to allow her husband to hold her hand when Early Truffle had ridden down, out of the blue, and made off with her and the payroll. He could just see it now: Rosa, full of umbrage, announcing to old Early, "Do you know who I am? Who my husband is?" Which, of course, was just too enticing for Early to pass up.

Batch of goddamn idiots, the lot of them.

"I have traced them as far as Crossed Spear," Madrid continued, oblivious. "There," he said, "they disappeared from sight. That is as much as I can help you."

"It's something, anyway," Fargo said. "Got a place to start."

For the first time since they had left his wife, Madrid smiled. He said, "For you, it will be enough. You have made quite a reputation since the old days. Now they call you the Trailsman, and you know the ways and languages of many peoples. I am proud, Skye Fargo, to call you my friend. I know you will do your best for me, and for Marga."

The next morning, Fargo set out for Crossed Spear. He figured he could make better time on the Ovaro, cutting a straight path to the mining town, instead of zigzagging all over hell and gone, following the stage route through the level places.

As he rode along, he thought over this mission he'd taken on, and the girl he was questing after.

Marga. An exotic name for an exotic-looking girl.

He'd forgotten to ask Madrid what color her eyes were. He guessed he'd have to settle for "light," for now.

And this "fancies the men too much"? Well, that was all kind of relative, wasn't it?

She couldn't fancy *every* man that crossed her path, or she would have married one of those arranged suitors Madrid mentioned. Some things were just plain subjective, and normal female longings might seem outrageous to an ice-queen sister like old Rosa.

After having met Rosa and spent a couple of days on the trail with her, he wouldn't be surprised if Madrid had to do a great deal of anvil lifting, just to keep from going loony.

And then he felt almost disappointed. He'd sort of been counting on this Marga being, as Madrid had said, a wanton. He'd pictured himself making his way back to Quake between heady bouts of quenching the carnal thirst of a beautiful, hot-to-trot female.

Almost disappointed?

Hell, he was heartbroken!

But still, he didn't waver from his course. Fargo being Fargo, he couldn't let a friend down.

He rode for five days, never stopping for the night in a town, where there might have been a friendly bed with soft sheets or a little earthy comfort. He slept in the open, rising at dawn and moving on, always moving on.

And at last, tired and dirty and hoping like hell that he could find a place to rinse out his bucks and get a bath, he came to the town of Crossed Spear.

It was almost dark and he decided, for once, to check into the hotel. He told himself that the Ovaro deserved deep straw and real hay, but the truth was that he wanted that bath. Besides, he had a few questions he wanted to ask around town.

After all, Marga had last been seen in these parts.

He figured that the ride here had just been the preliminaries. The real finding of Marga was just beginning.

After he got the Ovaro settled in at the local livery stable, he walked up to the hotel.

"Remember her?" he asked, flipping out the picture.

The desk clerk took a long look. Longer than he needed, really, but Fargo figured to let him drink in some of that beauty.

Finally, the clerk sighed. He was a skinny fellow, not more than twenty-two and over six feet tall, and put Fargo a little in mind of a scarecrow. The little wooden tag pinned to his shirt said, "Alfred Hastings, Night Manager."

Acne scars pocked young Mr. Hastings's hatchetlike face and he had nearly turned over the inkwell, almost stabbed himself with the letter opener, and did, in fact, shut his thumb in the cashbox during the few moments that Fargo had been standing there. Fargo figured looking at Marga's picture was as close as this poor kid was going to get to having himself a gal like Marga.

"Yeah," Hastings said, all moony, and still staring at Marga's unmoving, two-dimensional face. "I remember her, all right. I mean, holy smokes! Who could forget a gal like her? This picture sure don't do her any justice, though."

"When was she here?"

Hastings turned out to be a talker, and Fargo determined that the couple had been in town on the night he'd thought, and that they'd pulled out the next morning. The desk clerk didn't know where they'd gone, but he said they'd been on the outs while they were under his roof. He'd had to go knock on their door to quiet them down, and the woman, Marga, had broken a couple of figurines. Smashed them against the wall.

Terrific. thought Fargo. *She hurls things.*

"They still open next door?" he asked. He'd almost had to arm-wrestle the kid to get his picture back.

"The barbershop?" asked the boy, a little grumpily. "Yeah, Jess is open till eight." He screw up his face. "You gonna shave off that beard, Mister?"

"Nope. Want a bath, and then I want some dinner."

"That'd be Scott's Café, down the street," said Hastings. "Tell Marty I sent you."

"Fine," said Fargo. "And give me a room for later."

He inked his name on the register, passed his saddlebags over the front desk for safekeeping, and proceeded next door.

It wasn't any too soon. Those bucks were beginning to itch almost as much as his sense of curiosity.

Fighting, were they?

3

The bath left Fargo smelling much better, and dressed in his spare bucks. He'd given the old pair a good rinsing before rolling them up in towels to dry. The wash water had come away black, much to his chagrin.

Maybe he'd been a little hard on old Rosa Madrid, he thought, for not being more talkative. Maybe he ought to feel honored that she didn't wear a clothespin on her nose the whole way back.

Oh, hell.

It was dark, but he still made the rounds of places Marga and her fellow of the moment, Cort Cleveland, might have dropped in, where they might have mentioned something about their destination.

He had no luck at the mercantile or the dress shop—although he got a little wink and a lot of encouragement from Miss Darcy O'Connor, the proprietress.

He did no better at the tobacco shop, where he thought Cleveland might have stopped in for loose tobacco or cigars, or at the stage office itself.

The stationmaster remembered them coming in, all right, but hadn't seen them leave.

"And I see every single gosh-darned passenger, Mister," the old man had said, his freckled, hooked nose out of joint. "I'd sure as hell remember seein' *her* again!"

Disappointed, but hungry as a bear after a long winter's sleep, a rather dejected Fargo walked down to the café. He'd just started, he told himself. He'd check with the sheriff after supper. Something would turn up tomorrow if it didn't tonight.

But something had best turn up damned quick.

He ordered a big bowl of beef stew and a side of panfried potatoes, along with a beer and apple pie, for later. But they were all delivered to his table at one time, so he sat there, eating first a bit of stew, then one of pie, then one of spuds.

When he was finished, he ordered a second piece of pie—blueberry, this time—and coffee and sat there, thinking.

But before he had a chance to do much of it, a tall, skinny, older man in a black suit walked in and walked right over to his table. Fargo thought he looked like an undertaker as he stood there, hat in his hands, clearing his throat.

"Want something?" Fargo said. He wasn't exactly in the best of moods right now. His stew had been too salty, his potatoes too greasy, and his beer flat. The first piece of pie had been fair enough, but he was half afraid to drink the coffee.

The man cleared his throat. "Yes, indeed, sir," he said in a deep baritone voice. His breath carried the faint, stale smell of old whiskey.

"Allow me to introduce myself. I am Randall Ross, owner, editor, and proprietor of the *Crossed Spear Arrow*. I believe we may be able to work out an exchange of information."

Fargo's brow furrowed. "Maybe," he said. He gestured to the opposite chair. "Pull up a seat, Mr. Ross."

He pegged the newspaperman as a recent transplant to the western part of the continent, despite his age. Young men took off for the sunset country at the drop of a hat, but old men only went west when they had no other option. In passing, Fargo wondered what

Ross had done to whittle away his possibilities back east.

"Thank you, sir," Ross said. Looking relieved, he pulled out a chair. The relieved part surprised Fargo a little. Why would Ross think that Fargo wouldn't talk to him?

But he stuck out his hand, anyway, and Ross took it. "And you're Skye Fargo," Ross said, shaking Fargo's hand, slow and serious. "Why, I would have known you anyplace, sir."

When Fargo hiked his brow, Ross added, "You're quite famous, you know."

After easing his hand away, Fargo took a sip of his coffee. It was better than the beer, but that wasn't saying much. And he didn't much want to chat about how goddamn famous he was. "You wanted to trade some information, Mr. Ross?"

At last, out came the tablet and the lead stump, the tools of the trade of any reporter. Fargo figured that in a town this size, Mr. Randall Ross was the whole damned staff of the *Crossed Spear Arrow*, too. Probably even swept the place out.

The odor was stronger now that Ross was seated across from him, and it was Fargo's guess that Ross sent himself out for whiskey on a regular basis.

"Yes, indeed," Ross said, finding a fresh sheet in his notebook. "Information." He moistened the pencil on the tip of his tongue and began, "I understand that you are seeking a certain man and woman, Mr. Fargo."

"It's just Fargo," Fargo replied, cutting off a piece of pie with the side of his fork. "No 'Mister' to it." Ross had better get to the point quick, or get on his way. The stink of stale whiskey didn't exactly go with blueberries.

"Very well," said Ross. "I believe the gentleman in question was one Cort Cleveland, correct?"

Fargo nodded.

"Are you aware," Ross went on, "of Mr. Cleveland's past difficulties?"

Fargo swallowed. "Difficulties?" he asked. This was a new twist.

"Yes, indeed, Mr. Fargo. Sorry. Fargo," Ross said. "Legal difficulties, that is. Since Cleveland and the young lady—what was her name again?"

"Marga," Fargo said, then wished he hadn't, because Ross scribbled it down in his notebook.

"Yes," said Ross, "that was it. Since they left our fair city, I have done a little looking into Mr. Cleveland's past. My suspicions were raised when Mr. Cleveland got into a bit of an argument with our town sheriff. I believe something about Natchez, Mississippi, was mentioned."

This time, Fargo didn't really taste the coffee going down his throat. "Get to the point, Ross."

Ross leaned to the side in his chair and cocked his head. "In time, in time. An exchange of information, correct?"

Fargo didn't say anything.

"Now, could you tell me something about this young woman he's traveling with?" Ross went on. "She didn't seem too happy to be with him, but then, one doesn't always give much heed to what women want. They are generally such flighty creatures."

"She's unhappy?" Fargo asked. Maybe she wouldn't have much of a problem, after all. He'd pictured himself having to carry her off over his shoulder, like a kicking, screaming sack of potatoes, and having to fend off Cleveland, too.

"It was my impression," Ross said with a shrug. Clearly he had only been an observer, and not a player in the situation. "When they left town, she didn't appear to be a delighted participant."

"When did they leave?" Fargo asked.

"Tell me about her," Ross said, leaning forward.

"She's the sister-in-law of a friend of mine," Fargo

said with a sigh. "She disappeared from home. I'm tracking her."

It wasn't much, but it was all he was prepared to give. He didn't think Madrid would be too happy to have his dirty laundry dragged all over the streets of Crossed Spear, New Mexico, and God only knows where else.

"This friend hired you?"

Fargo sighed again. "Did Cleveland say where they were headed?"

"Who's your friend, Mr. Fargo?" Ross asked.

Now it was Fargo's turn to lean forward, but he did so in a much more threatening manner than had Ross, and Ross shrank back a bit.

"Listen, Mr. Randall Ross, I'm through dancin' with you," Fargo said, and there was a definite threat in his voice. "Where'd they go?"

"Cheney," Ross answered, his Adam's apple suddenly bobbing nervously. "They went to Cheney."

"And this Cleveland feller that she's with," Fargo went on. "What's his story?"

"That's not his real name," Ross answered. He appeared to be regaining some of his composure. Although it was relatively straight to begin with, he restraightened his tie and cleared his throat. "Really, Fargo, I thought we could do an even trade. Tit for tat, as it were."

"I told you, her name's Marga—she's the sister of a friend, and that I've been hired to find her and bring her back," Fargo said. He was ready to reach out and grab Ross by the collar if need be. "That's three or four things you didn't know, and as many that I didn't need to tell you. You told me they're going to Cheney. Seems like you owe me about three, there, Ross. I'll let it go at two if they're juicy ones."

Ross sat back in his chair with a thump and snidely said, "So gunmen can count, after all."

"Up to six, anyway," Fargo replied. He didn't crack a smile. "You didn't get near that, yet. Now, if you don't mind, Mister, I'd like to know what you dug up about this Cleveland. And you could toss in tellin' me which day they left."

"I told you, Cleveland's not his real name," Ross said, with a great deal of righteous indignation for a man who stank. "I couldn't find out his true name, just the five or six aliases he's used before. Travels as a salesman, but he's more along the lines of a confidence man." He stopped and stared at Fargo. "And they left three days ago, on horseback. Happy?"

Fargo pushed his chair back with a scrape. "You know," he said, tossing his napkin to the table, "you don't have much respect for us so-called famous gunmen. Either that, or you've got a whole lot of gravel on you. Which I doubt. But one way or the other, I don't think you're gonna live too long out here. Take my advice. Go on back to Boston or New York or wherever you came from. Whatever's back there can't be worse than what'll happen to you if you stick around here."

He picked up the bundle of damp towels that contained his wet bucks, turned on his heel, tossed a silver dollar on the counter, and walked out the door.

He walked back to the hotel, inwardly grumbling about newspapermen in general, and this one in particular, but at least he'd come away with more than he had when he came into town.

Marga and Cleveland were on the outs, and they were fighting.

Cleveland was a con man. Had Marga just found out? Maybe. Or maybe she was mad because Cort Cleveland wasn't his real name. Or maybe she knew nothing, and was just mad on general principle. He'd known women like that.

It didn't really matter. He just hoped she'd stay mad. She'd be easier to coax into coming home, then.

And they'd gone to Cheney, on horseback.

Well, that wasn't bad. Cheney wasn't more than a day's ride, and it was little more than a wide spot in the road. Folks there would be apt to remember every detail of a stranger's visit.

Especially a stranger as beautiful as Marga.

And just then, right at that exact moment, Fargo realized that he didn't know her last name.

Madrid hadn't offered it, and her maiden name had never come up with his wife. Not that much of anything had come up as a topic for discussion so far as Rosa was concerned.

Shaking his head and muttering under his breath, he pushed open the door to the hotel. Some big, famous tracker he was!

There was a different fellow at the front desk this time, and again, Fargo went through the drill. Had he seen this lady? Had he seen her man? Did he know where they'd gone, and had he overheard them talking?

This clerk had been employed at the hotel for only two days, and had seen neither hide nor hair of Marga or her con man. Nothing came of it, other than the clerk getting his eye full of Marga's picture. In fact, Fargo practically had to wrench it away.

He wandered upstairs and found his room, then spent the next five minutes deliberating about finding the sheriff. At last, he decided against it. He'd likely only find a night deputy on duty, anyhow.

He'd go in the morning.

He wasn't all that sleepy, though.

Leaving his bucks in the room, he went back downstairs and out the door. He found himself a pretty little whore named Sweet Pea over at the saloon, and convinced her to come back to the hotel with him.

Actually, she didn't take much convincing.

"Sweet Pea," he said as he helped her out of her clothes. "I'm inclined to believe you're a very bad girl."

25

"Inclined to agree, Mister," she said with a smile as she eagerly tugged down his britches. She was a red-head, and she was a real one, Fargo noted. "You want me on my back or what?"

"Or what," Fargo replied, backing her up against the wall. He was already swollen and hard as a rock. "For starters."

Sweet Pea giggled as he lifted her up, and locked her legs around his waist as he entered her. She let out a little sigh.

"Sweet Pea, I believe you've done this before," he said.

"Once or twice," she replied with a hint of a smile.

"Well, you're gonna triple your count before the night's over, honey," Fargo said. With both hands cupping her nice, fat bottom, he began to get to work.

And it's a damn fine kind of work, he thought, *if you can get it.*

Right after breakfast, Fargo made his way up the street to the jail. But the sheriff was no more help than the second desk clerk had been.

Mostly, he complained about his sciatica.

And so Fargo lit out for Cheney. He'd been through it about five or six years ago. The town hadn't impressed him much when he was there before, and he didn't expect it to impress him this time.

He wondered, as he rode the Ovaro down the rutted and weedy trail to Cheney, what in the world a girl like Marga had ever seen in a man like Cort Cleveland. She'd likely been conned as much as any snake oil patron or victim of the badger game.

And he found himself taking out that framed photograph several times, just to look at her. God, she was beautiful! Those eyes, those wonderful eyes . . .

He shook his head. He was going plumb crazy, that's what! Even last night, he'd called Sweet Pea

"Marga" a couple of times. She'd been a good sport about it, but Jesus!

Snorting derisively at himself—and women, in general—he shoved the picture back in his pocket and rode on.

4

He got to Cheney at about midafternoon, and tethered the Ovaro to the hitching rail outside the sheriff's office. If you could call it that. Cheney's answer to a jail was a corner of the town's only saloon, which had been rigged with a sort of wooden, man-sized cage just big enough for a cot and the space to pace beside it. Fargo thought it must be real entertaining for the locals when they had a man in there.

Right at the moment, it was blessedly vacant.

As was the saloon. The only man in the place was a balding, bored-looking bartender, who was slouched against the bar, lackadaisically polishing a glass, until he saw Fargo.

"Help you, Mister?" he said, straightening.

Fargo bellied up to the bar. "Yeah," he said. "Beer. And a little information, if you've got time."

"Sure," the bartender said with a hint of a smile. "Ain't got much else around here." He drew the beer, then slid it toward Fargo, slopping foam. "What's on your mind, stranger?"

Fargo stuck out his hand. "Name's Fargo."

The bartender took it and gave it a terse shake, saying, "Joe Forester."

"Glad to meet you, Forester." Fargo reached for

his pocket. "I'm trailing a couple of folks. This is the woman." He slid the framed picture across the bar. "She's with a fella. Tall, blond, might say he's a drummer. Her name's Marga, his is Cort Cleveland. Although he might be using an alias."

Joe Forester picked up the picture and stared, pursing his lips. Then he burst into a full-blown, drawn-out whistle. "Holy Christ. She's sure a looker, ain't she?"

"That she is," Fargo replied, fending off a tinge of jealousy. Actually, he wanted nothing more than to slap the picture out of the barkeep's hands.

"What you want them folks for, anyhow?" There was an accusation in there, somewhere.

Fargo was getting used to it. When people saw how beautiful Marga was, they were all of a sudden on her side, no matter what.

"Her brother-in-law hired me," he explained. "She ran off with this fella, and it's come to the brother-in-law's attention that maybe this fella isn't everything he claimed to be. I'm supposed to check up on her, make sure she's all right."

It was close enough, and it satisfied the barkeep.

Joe Forester never took his eyes from the picture, though. "I can see why he'd be concerned about her," he muttered.

Then, at last, he tore his gaze away and looked up at Fargo. "I wasn't lucky enough to see her in the flesh, but there was a feller through here a few days back that might be this man you're lookin' for. Cort Somebody, you say?"

Fargo nodded.

"Didn't catch his name," Joe said. "He didn't throw one, come to think of it. Sat over yonder for about an hour, playin' cards with Tom Beck and Clancy Yeager." He poked his thumb toward a corner opposite the makeshift cell.

"Tom Beck and Clancy Yeager?" Fargo said.

"Where could I find them?" He took back the photograph and slid it into his pocket. For a second, he thought that Joe was going to dive in there after it.

But Joe only sighed and said, "You won't find Tom. He's out on the range somewhere by now. Now, old Clancy, you can dig up easy enough. He's the law around these parts. Oughta be back in a few minutes, if'n you want to wait."

"Be pleased," replied Fargo, and moseyed on over to a table.

He sat there, making small talk with Joe, until the sheriff staggered in. Fargo knew he was the sheriff only because of the tin badge pinned crookedly on the man's chest. Clancy Yeager had every appearance of being the town drunk, rather than the town law.

Turned out that he only looked that way, though. Sheriff Yeager was as sober as a judge underneath those ratty clothes and his odd way of walking.

The barkeep made the introductions.

"I ain't soused" were the first words out of Yeager's mouth.

"Never said you were," said Fargo, holding out his hand.

"Got me a nervous condition," Yeager said as he shook hands. He scraped back a chair. "Makes me a little gamey on the walk. Can't run for beans, neither."

Fargo wanted to remark that Yeager was just plain gamey, period, but held his tongue. About that, anyway. He leaned back in his chair, twirled his beer, and asked his questions.

"Yup," said the sheriff, nodding. "That was him, all right. Knew he had a woman with him, but only saw her backside when they was ridin' out of town. Chestnut and a bay, you said?"

Fargo nodded. He'd found out that much at the livery in Crossed Spear. Cleveland had paid cash for them, and two saddles, too, with no quibbling, despite the inflated price—in Fargo's opinion, anyway—that the stableman had charged.

"Can't say as I liked him much," the sheriff went on. "Kind of a greasy feller, if you know what I mean. Slippery, like. From what you say, I guess he is."

"Appreciate the information, sheriff."

From behind the bar, Joe piped up, "Take a look at the picture, Clancy!"

"What picture?"

Fargo produced the little frame once again, and slid it across the table.

"Holy crud," muttered the sheriff as he picked it up. "By God, I sure wish she'd turned around when they was leaving. I woulda liked to have seen her face in person. Now, that's the stuff of an old man's dreams!"

"Middle-aged man's, too," added Joe.

"Yeah," said Fargo wearily. "It's that. Now, did Cleveland say where they were going next?"

Fargo kept on the move. He followed them from town to town, always a few days behind. Marga seemed to have all but disappeared, since nobody since the town of Crossed Spear had actually seen her. She rode into town with Cleveland, and she sat in the hotel, period.

It didn't sound like the behavior he'd expect from Marga, the man magnet, and he was more and more suspicious of Cleveland. In fact, he had just about talked himself into believing that Marga was truly traveling against her will.

It only made him move faster.

He went from Cheney to Hastings, from Hastings to Apache Springs, from Apache Springs to Sprewlock, and from Sprewlock to Bent Fork, making up the time between himself and Cort Cleveland by not spending the night in either Hastings or Sprewlock. By the time he rode from Bent Fork to Silver Mount, he was within a day of them.

He asked the usual questions at the livery, the sheriff's office, the saloon, and the hotel. Again, he was told that Marga never came out, that she was only spotted at the livery and the hotel, but that Cleveland had stopped in at the saloon for a little poker.

Again, he hadn't played too long. Only an hour or so. Cleveland was showing all the signs of a born gambler trying to taper off gradually. Fargo expected to hear, any minute, that in one of these towns along the way Cleveland's gambling dam had broken, and that he'd sat in at the card table for a twenty-four-hour stretch. That's usually how it was with these boys.

But so far, Cleveland was on his good behavior.

And at least, Marga wasn't scuffed up. He'd made a point of asking about that at the livery and the hotel. No visible bruises or abrasions. At least, Cleveland wasn't hitting her.

But the desk clerk at Hastings and the clerk at Apache Springs had both said that Cleveland and Marga had fought. Both reported shouting and breaking of the bric-a-brac, and both clerks had to go to Cleveland's room and knock at the door after complaints from other lodgers. Somebody had thrown a little piece of pottery at the clerk's voice in Hastings.

He said he had jumped a foot and a half back from the closed door.

Well, old Marga wasn't going quietly—that was for sure.

He had worked his way across New Mexico, and halfway into the territory called Arizona, and Cleveland showed no signs of stopping. Fargo wondered if Cleveland was going to "west" himself right smack through California and into the Pacific Ocean.

And Fargo also wondered why Marga hadn't taken advantage of those hourlong poker breaks of Cleveland's to make her own break for it.

You'd think that even if she didn't want to get away from him, a girl like her would have stopped in at a milliner's shop or something! Hell, she likely couldn't go a day without buying some kind of frilly little doodad or other.

So why was she doing without, all of a goddamn sudden?

She never even went out for meals. Cleveland did, though. He always made at least one appearance at the local restaurant or café, and ordered a second meal, which he carried out with him.

The way Fargo figured it, the only way a little spitfire like Marga would stay in that room, and put up with this nonsense, was if Cleveland kept her bound and gagged most of the time.

But then, why did she always leave town with him so quietly? Why did she seem to just go along with everything?

It was a puzzlement, and one which had been rubbing Fargo's psyche raw.

For his part, he was about to rub hollows into that picture frame. He'd taken to studying it at night, sometimes sitting up till after eleven with it in his lap, just thinking.

He really had to get hold of himself, he thought. But he still kept taking that picture out.

It was while he was in Silver Mount—loitering over a pretty decent piece of peach pie and trying to decide whether or not to take a chance on a cloudy sky and a quarter moon that night—that he got a surprise.

He was in the back of the café, sitting against a wall and facing the door, when suddenly, the door flew open and a man fell in, backside first. Fargo—along with half the other customers—jumped to his feet automatically.

Merely on reflex, he had halfway drawn his gun, when the man, still skidding to a halt, shouted, "Goddamn it, you walleyed greaser!" and scrambled to his feet. He bolted back out the door without a word—or a backward glance—to any of the patrons.

Fargo didn't need anybody to tell him who that was. He would have recognized that slab-sided, gravel-voiced son of a bitch anywhere: Owen Thurst.

As he sat back down, he was torn between finishing his pie and finishing Owen. The pie won. Besides, he figured maybe that the fellow Owen was fighting with would do it for him.

Now, Owen had been a thorn in Fargo's side for a good long time, ever since Fargo had outbid Owen for the affections of a little gal down in Mexico. Outbid? Hell, Fargo hadn't needed to offer a nickel!

But Owen wouldn't let it go. About a year later, when Fargo was hired to bring him to the law over in Texas, Owen's grudge got a whole lot bigger and a whole lot nastier, too. Owen had escaped the Texas jail Fargo delivered him to, killing a deputy and wounding an unlucky store clerk during the break, and had come straight after Fargo.

Now, it wasn't Fargo's fault that Owen had a proclivity for holding up stages. And it also wasn't his fault that he'd been the one hired to go find Owen and bring him back.

Although he would have volunteered for it, if anybody had asked him.

Owen was about as high up on Fargo's list as was the scum that grew on tank water when the temperature rose too high. He was just about that slimy, too.

Well, Owen had come after Fargo, and Fargo had ended up shooting him in the leg. Owen went to the doc's office and then to the jail and eventually prison, and Fargo went on his way.

And now it looked as if old Owen was out again, and spoiling for bear.

But Fargo wasn't going to be the bear this time, he decided, as he pushed his empty pie plate away. Owen was more trouble than he was worth, and Fargo was awfully damn close to Marga. He wasn't going to let her slip away on account of a lousy piece of pond scum.

So he stood up, stretched, paid his tab, and then slid out the front door.

Owen—and whoever Owen had been fighting with—was long gone and it was all the way dark. Too dark, Fargo decided, to travel. The clouds had moved in to cover the scant moon, and there was no way he'd take a chance on banging up the Ovaro by trying to ride him through the desert in darkness.

So he walked on up to the telegrapher's office, sent Madrid a wire—which he'd done sporadically, ever since setting out after Marga—and started back to the hotel, always keeping an eye peeled for Owen.

It was just as he'd reached the lobby and was putting a boot on the stairs that, from behind him, he heard Owen's unmistakable roar.

"Fargo!" Owen shouted angrily. As if he knew any other way to shout. "Skye Fargo, you stinkin' horse turd!"

Fargo heard the cock of a gun's hammer and froze. He needed this right now like a gopher needs a pocket watch. He didn't turn around so much as a hair, though. He stood there, one foot on the first riser, and said, "Evening, Owen."

Owen didn't answer, and finally Fargo turned his head in Owen's direction. "What's the matter, Owen? Aren't you glad to see me?"

The desk clerk, who had dropped to the floor behind his counter at Owen's entrance, had yet to resurface. And the gravel-voiced Owen Thurst, hardly a quick study on the best of days, scrunched up his weather-beaten features almost comically.

"Well, of course, I ain't glad!" he said, still pointing the gun. "Why? Did you expect me to be?"

Fargo shrugged. "Didn't expect anything, one way or the other."

"Well, prepare to be shot dead," Owen said theatrically.

Fargo waved a hand, but high enough so that Owen wouldn't mistake it as a grab for his gun. "Now, Owen," he said, "Why would you want to go and do a stupid thing like that? I'm not carryin' any paper on you." And then Fargo frowned. "Should I be?"

Owen stood there a minute, taking in what Fargo had asked him. "No. Course not! I'm law abidin'. Ask anybody."

"I wonder what that fella you were beating on when you went through the café door would say to that," Fargo noted, scratching the back of his head.

"Aw, I weren't . . . Was you there?" Owen asked, and for a second Fargo considered saying no, he was in the next town, but then, Owen might consider him a witch or a psychic and shoot him on general principles. If, indeed, he knew what general principles were.

So he said, "That I was, Owen. I'd know that sandpaper voice of yours anywhere. But if you don't mind, I'm on my way up to get some sleep. I'm cutting out first thing in the morning."

"T-that's right, sir," said a voice from behind the desk. It was the desk clerk, who was still on the floor. "He's goin' all right. Told me so when he checked in. You don't want to get blood all over my boss's lobby, now do you?"

"That's right, Owen," Fargo said. "Why get the law after you again when you're doing so well at being law-abiding?" He made a mental note to do something nice for that desk clerk.

"Why, if you shot me," Fargo went on, "you'd have to shoot him." He hiked a thumb in the direction of the desk. "And if you shot him, why, the whole goddamn town would get into an uproar. He's the mayor's son, you know."

Now, Fargo didn't know any such thing. But, God bless him, the clerk went along with it.

"That's right," said his disembodied voice. "My daddy's Mr. Hiram Q. Lynch, our town mayor and a territorial justice of the peace."

Fargo shook his head. "Be a bad thing, Owen."

The nose of Owen's pistol started to droop, and the thought flickered across his face at the same rate his poor brain was probably processing it. It was a long wait.

But finally, he holstered his gun.

"Well, shit," he said.

Fargo nodded. "You've got a way with words, there, Owen."

"Shut up, Fargo," Owen grumbled.

The desk clerk started to stand up, and peeked over the rim of the counter.

" 'Night, Owen," Fargo said. "You, too, Percy," he added to the clerk. "My regards to your father."

"Yes, sir, Mr. Fargo," the clerk said, and stood the rest of the way up. He cast a glance toward Owen, who was backing toward the door, and added, "I'll be sure to tell him."

"Good boy," Fargo said, never missing a beat as he heard the hotel's door slam behind Owen Thurst. He walked to his room, and as he slid the key into the door, he muttered, "Why do I think that I haven't heard the last of you, you stupid son of a bitch?"

5

Owen Thurst rode slowly and carefully out of town, picking his way through the moonless desert. His horse stumbled a few times and almost went down once—for which Owen lashed it with his reins—but he finally made it to camp.

Red Neal was still up, and not in the best of moods. "Where the hell you been?" he demanded, before Owen was even off his horse. "I waited supper on you!"

Owen swung down to the ground and led his horse toward Red's. "You sound like an old woman," he said.

Red scowled, then spat for good measure. Owen saw to his horse. There was no further conversation until Owen slumped down in his bedroll, beside the fire.

"Light's nice," he said, reaching for his fixing pouch. He began to roll a smoke. "Darker than the inside of a black sow's belly out there."

Red, it appeared, was not talking to him. Owen might not have been the sharpest tool in the shed, but he was far ahead of Red. He had to stay on Red's good side, because when Red was happy, Red would do just about anything Owen wanted. And Red was just about the only person in the whole wide world who didn't hate the sight of him.

So Owen said, "Sorry, Red." He stuck the smoke between his lips, and said, "What'd you fix, anyhow?"

Still, Red was silent, damn it. The son of a bitch had gone into another one of his pouts. He was more trouble sometimes than having a woman along!

For a second, Owen considered just sticking out his boot and gouging Red in the shins, but thought better of it. After all, there was just about no better shot than Red, when he was in the mood. And he couldn't a find more trusty backup.

Owen lit his smoke, letting Red stew for a second. He blew out a long plume of yellowish smoke—he didn't exactly buy the best tobacco—and then he said, "I beat me up a Mexican. Damned beaner. And I run into somebody at the hotel."

He picked up the coffee pot off the fire, but it was empty.

Red looked up, his eye narrowed. "Why'd you go to the hotel?" he said. "You didn't have no business there. No business I know of, anyhow."

As patiently as he could—which wasn't any too patient—Owen said, "I was up there because this feller told me that the beaner—the one I was beatin' on—had run in there. Turned out he was wrong. There weren't no beaner in there. But somebody else was."

He paused for dramatic effect. Red was leaning forward a little, so Owen figured he'd hooked him, all right.

At last, old Red couldn't stand the silence anymore, because he demanded, "Well? You gonna tell me who it was?"

Whack! Just like a rat in a trap. Owen smiled.

"Red, you ever hear me tell about a feller named Fargo?"

Red snorted. "You joshin' me? About every other day, that's all!"

"Well, he was in town, right in that hotel lobby."
He had Red's attention now. With supper forgotten,
Red looked at him eagerly.

"You gun him down?" Red asked eagerly. "You
shoot him dead?"

It was Owen's turn to scowl. "Naw. There was too
many people around. Too many witnesses, you know?
You got any more coffee?"

Red nodded, in his best imitation of a sage. Owen
wasn't sure which query that nod answered, but went
on, anyway.

"I asked a couple of questions on my way out, and
he's leavin' in the morning," Owen said. "Goin' southwest, to Quartzite. And we're goin' southwest, too."

Red's face, intent before, now widened into a hope-
ful grin. "We're gonna gun him, ain't we, Owen? Hell,
my trigger finger's gone all to itch! When you figure
we'll catch up with him? You think maybe we could
lay a trap ahead of him?"

Red was big on strategy.

Most of which didn't work out. None of it, come to
think of it.

But Owen let him enjoy the moment and revel in
his supposed craftiness. He leaned back on his elbow,
grimaced, then shifted. That damn beaner had caught
him a good one in the ribs. He'd be bruised tomorrow
if he wasn't already. He spent a few moments silently
cursing the whole race of Mexicans, only to be interrupted by Red, who was suddenly looking a little
worried.

" 'Xactly how fast you think this Fargo feller is,
Owen?"

Owen pursed his lips. "How fast? Real fast. The
fastest." And then he hurriedly added, "But not as
fast as you, Red. I never in all my born days seen
anybody as fast as you."

Red's smile returned. "Then I'll get him for you,
Owen. You just find him, and I'll get him."

40

Owen stubbed out his smoke. "That I will."

"He won't trouble you no more," Red said.

"I got that, Red."

"He'll be deader'n a door mouse."

"Door*nail*. And that's good, Red."

"Deader than a—"

"Red?" Owen broke in. Like he always had to.

"What, Owen?"

"You gonna make any more coffee? I could sure use me a cup."

The next morning, Fargo was up before the dawn. Chewing on a chunk of jerky, he rode out of town just as the first soft fingers of the morning sun were creeping over the horizon.

He wanted to get on to Quartzite and hopefully, finally, catch up with Marga and Cleveland. Especially Marga.

But he also wanted to avoid another run-in with Owen Thurst. Owen wasn't too quick on the take, but Owen was as single-minded as all get-out. Fargo wasn't laboring under any delusions. He knew that if Owen could figure out where he was going, Owen would be there, too.

And, more than likely, try to put a slug in his back.

Gosh, he thought dryly. *That sounds like a whole heap of fun.*

He should have stayed in town and waited out Owen Thurst. Actually, he should have taken care of him last night, he supposed. But there was something decidedly against his nature, and code, to shoot a man right in the middle of a hotel lobby, even if Owen had been holding a gun on him. And Owen hadn't fired first, had he?

Stupid code.

He should have just shot Owen last night. Not killed him, but put him out of commission.

Hell, the sheriff was probably looking for him, any-

41

way. Men like Owen couldn't seem to keep away from trouble, and jails—the same way that flies can't help being attracted to molasses, or moths to a lamp flame.

Fargo shook his head angrily. There was more than likely a reward out on old Owen, as well, he figured. He could have gotten rid of him and laid his hands on a little spare cash at the same time.

Now, why the hell hadn't he thought of that last night?

Because he was thinking about Marga, he told himself. He'd been thinking about her when he should have been tending to business.

Well, Marga *was* his business. Strictly business. He just had to remember that.

And he did a fairly decent job of it.

He didn't pull out her picture again and stare at it, like a lovesick puppy, until he stopped to rest the Ovaro at midday.

Marga tried to scream at him, but Cleveland clapped a hand over her face before she could get any sound out.

So she did what she'd done before, and what any red-blooded, half-Spanish, half-English girl would do under the circumstances—she bit him.

This time, it was Cleveland who hollered.

Marga slipped away, to the other side of the hotel room. A smile was on her lips but her eyes were narrowed, her nose in the air, her body posture stiff.

"Did I draw blood?" she asked sweetly. Her tongue searched the inside of her mouth for a coppery trace.

"Goddamn it!" Cleveland said, pulling out a handkerchief, with which he proceeded to swathe his hand. She thought she saw a hint of red. "You know you did, you crazy cat!" he half-shouted.

"Meow," said Marga.

Cleveland raised a bandaged hand. "I oughta . . ."

"Get the horses?" Marga asked innocently. "It's already past ten."

Cleveland mumbled a terse "Shit!" He grabbed his hat off the peg on the wall. "You and your goddamned plan. I shoulda seen it coming."

"But you didn't," she said coyly. "You didn't at all, my dear Cort. Now get the horses like a good boy." She sank into a chair and demurely crossed her legs. "I don't feel like walking all the way down to that filthy livery."

Cleveland snorted, but left at last, slamming the door behind him.

"Good riddance," Marga whispered, and reached for her bag, from which she took a silver cigar case. The cigars in it were very slim, very narrow, and she took one out and lit it, puffing little white clouds of smoke toward the ceiling.

She posed, unconsciously, as she sat there. Marga was astoundingly beautiful, and she knew it. She'd played on it all her life. She lifted a hand and calmly stroked her hair into place. Today, she had let it hang in soft ebony waves that fell down around her neck and shoulders, and cascaded down her back like a river. A river of night, someone had once called it. Was it a trail hand? A store keeper?

Anyway, it was wholly poetic.

A woman's hair was her crowning glory, Mama had always said.

Cort liked it, too. Idly, she wondered just how deeply her teeth had sunk into his hand. She hadn't felt bone. Pity.

"Ah, Cort, Cort, Cort," she murmured as she smoked. She sent a smoke ring, perfect, toward the ceiling. "Such a fool."

Her smile widened and turned just a tad predatory. "But such a handsome fool . . ."

* * *

43

Owen and Red, who hadn't started out nearly as early as Fargo, had bypassed town and were now south of it by about five miles.

Owen had been doing some thinking. He'd been thinking quite a bit about seeing Fargo dead, and he'd been thinking about watching Red do it. Both those things gave him a tremendous amount of pleasure, yes indeed!

But he'd also been thinking about Red, all by himself.

Red was getting worse. Owen didn't think that just dumbness, by itself, ever got any worse or any better, for that matter. But Red seemed to get more and more like a dog and less like a man with each passing week. He half expected to wake up one fine morning and find Red sitting there, panting and scratching his ear with his foot.

'Course, mayhap it was his imagination. Things were, sometimes.

Red was awfully eager, though. Awfully eager to do whatever would please Owen, awfully eager to do what he was told. And that deal last night, about Owen having missed supper!

Now, that beat everything, didn't it?

God, it was almost like traveling with a woman. Now, that chilled Owen to the bone—the thought of having a female sidekick, that is. He couldn't imagine anything worse than that for a rough-and-tumble man's man like himself.

Well, Red wasn't a female, but he was just as possessive, just as nervous, and just as crazy as one. Owen figured that Red's time—as his traveling companion, anyway—was coming to an end. Red would do anything for him, Owen knew. But there came a time, goddammit!

Yessir, there came a time.

It wouldn't be until Red killed Fargo, though. As

crazy as Red was making him lately, Red could stay around till after he'd done his little job.

But then? Look out.

In his sleep, Owen thought. *That's when I'll do it.* He knew Red—and Red's skills—too well to even imagine that he could draw and fire as fast as Red could. He wasn't that much of a fool.

So he'd wait until after Red had shot Fargo for him, and then he'd creep up on him one night, while he was dozing in his bedroll . . .

"Owen," said Red, and Owen nearly jumped out of the saddle.

"What?" he snapped, embarrassed.

But if Red had noticed, he didn't give any sign. "Owen," he said, "tell me that Fargo story again. You know, about how he crossed you, and how you was so brave and all."

Owen considered. "All right, Red."

He launched into the tale of his capture—and then his recapture—by Fargo, the son-of-a-bitching bastard, and while he was telling it, he found himself having second thoughts.

After all, he wouldn't likely find another fellow who'd listen so eagerly, would he? When he was riding with Sam Peck—why, Peck had put a slug clean through his leg after just a week and a half of that story.

Well, if Red was starting to act like a dog, maybe he could be trained.

That gave Owen a chuckle, and he almost laughed out loud, right in the middle of telling about how he bravely escaped from that stupid jail—which was normally one of his favorite parts.

Red, trained to sit and fetch, maybe to sit up and beg.

Now that would sure be a laugh, wouldn't it?

6

Fargo rode into Quartzite at about midafternoon, and checked around town before he even put up the Ovaro at the livery.

As it turned out, he was glad he hadn't invested in a stall and feed. Between the hotel clerk, the sheriff, and the liveryman, he determined that Marga and Cleveland had left town at around ten thirty, and that they were headed toward Pine Ridge.

He had left New Mexico proper behind and was now in the Arizona Territory, which was brash and new, and without the charm of the old New Mexico towns, with a few exceptions. Pine Ridge wasn't one of them, either. He'd been there once, just when the town was starting, and frankly, he was surprised it was still there.

Pine Ridge was, as he recalled, a small mass of buildings huddled in a valley in the foothills of the White Mountains. They didn't have any silver or gold to mine, and the land was too hilly and poor for cattle—or any other livestock, for that matter.

He couldn't think of a damned reason why anybody would want to live there in the first place, let alone try to make a living there.

But apparently somebody was.

He walked past the saloon, begrudging himself the

time to stop in for one drink, and went back up to the sheriff's office, where he'd tied the Ovaro to the rail. The sheriff had been no help whatsoever in tracking down Marga and Cleveland. There'd been the usual ruckus at the hotel and the usual gape-mouthed stableman, but the sheriff hadn't known a damned thing.

When he got to the jail, the sheriff was sitting out on the sidewalk in his rocking chair, his boots up on the rail.

"Find who you was lookin' for?" he asked lazily.

"Nope," replied Fargo. He unwound the Ovaro's reins. "Found out where they were going, though."

"Fargo?" the sheriff added.

"What?"

"Don't be comin' through my town again."

Fargo stared at him, his eyes narrowing slightly. He could set this sheriff straight about just who he should let ride through his town and who he shouldn't, but decided against it. He had to be on the move. Besides, this fool of a lawman might just arrest him to make a point.

He said, "Fine with me," and swung up into the Ovaro's saddle.

"Fargo?" the sheriff called from his chair, just as Fargo was reining away.

"What?"

"If'n you want to travel quiet, you'd best get rid of that loud horse," the sheriff said. "I didn't recognize you when you come in, but the second I saw that paint of yours . . ."

Fargo didn't say anything, just nodded, and quietly jogged on out of town. Get rid of the Ovaro, his ass! He'd bet his saddle that there wasn't any paper on him in the whole of the Arizona Territory, either. Some people just went power-crazy when you let them pin a badge on their shirts—that was all.

He rode up in altitude as he went to the south, then the west, then the south again. He paced the Ovaro, loping for a time, then bringing him down into a comfortable jog, and then walking before he stopped to rest. Then he urged the Ovaro into a fast trot before he let him lope again.

He was about five miles out of Pine Ridge, and just getting ready for his second stop, when the sun went down. But there were no clouds tonight, not a one. The fat crescent moon wasn't putting out much light, but he had the aid of the stars. And the road—it was almost an actual road, by now—was clear.

He decided to go on.

He kept the Ovaro to a careful walk—so careful, in fact, that the horse was bobbing his head and fighting the restraining bit for the last two miles of it. But he pulled into Lopez right about two hours later.

Leaving the Ovaro at the livery and showing the photograph to the stable hand—who nodded enthusiastically and said, yes, they'd come in that afternoon, and then pointed to their horses—he anxiously walked up to the hotel.

Surprisingly, the town had grown a good bit since he'd been there. What had been a smallish clump of buildings, seemingly huddled tight against the mountains, had grown into what Fargo considered a real town.

The desk clerk at the hotel confirmed it, and added that the reason for the recent growth was a small silver strike, just out of town.

"Not enough to bring in more than one minin' concern," the clerk said with a shrug, "but one's enough to grow this here ol' town."

Fargo brought out the picture, and gave its glass a rub before he handed it over. The stableman had dirty hands, and had smudged it.

"Seen her?" Fargo asked in a low tone, and leaned across the desk. "Her name's Marga, and she's travelin' with a man named Cleveland. Cort Cleveland."

The clerk stared at the photograph and smiled.

"She's a real looker, ain't she? Purty enough to be an actress." Reluctantly, he handed the picture back. "Yeah, she's here. They come in a few hours ago. What you want 'em for, anyhow?"

Fargo went through his old song and dance once more, which seemed to satisfy the clerk. It was amazing how, whenever he made inquiries, the fellow he was asking was suddenly on Marga's side, suddenly protective of her. Fargo wondered how they would have reacted if she'd been ugly or fat or old.

It was a moot point. Marga was what she was, and that was the reaction he was getting. He should be used to it by this time.

"They're in Room Five," the clerk added, "if you want to see 'em."

Fargo hesitated. If Cleveland was in fact holding Marga against her will, he'd do better than to burst in and grab her. He decided to wait. Cleveland would go out to play cards, if he were true to form. Fargo could go in, then. Besides, he suspected that Cleveland was hogtying her to get her to stay.

"Oh, tomorrow will do just fine," Fargo lied. "I'm too tuckered to see about it now. Just gonna go up and fall down on the bed." His eyes narrowed. "You got good mattresses?"

"Yes, sir!" the clerk offered. "Best in town!"

Fargo figured that probably wasn't any too good, but didn't say anything. He signed the register, right under Mr. and Mrs. Cort Cleveland, and found that it put up the hairs on his neck. If Cleveland had actually married her . . .

No, he thought. *That's crazy.*

But that jealousy still worked at him.

He picked up his saddlebags and mounted the stairs.

He was in Number Seven, right next door to their room, which was lucky. The moment he closed his door behind him and lit a lamp, he put an ear to the common wall and listened for any sound.

But there wasn't a peep out of them, even though he knew they were in there. Not a word, nothing. Not even anybody snoring.

Odd, he thought.

He didn't unpack his saddlebags. He pulled out a chuck of jerky and gnawed at it, staving off his hunger pains for the time being. He couldn't stave off this nervousness, though.

"Get a grip on yourself, Fargo," he muttered. "You've got to get this girl first. You can't go falling in love with Marga when you don't even know her."

But in a way, he had. He had fallen right into that picture, those eyes, that hair, that tight-lipped, Mona Lisa smile, and he'd fallen in love, goddammit.

That was the power of Marga's beauty, he guessed. She could make everybody who saw her fall head over heels without even trying. And he told himself to knock it off, cut it out, leave it behind.

He had a job to do.

And as to anything else? Well, he could worry about that later.

Still, it made him feel kind of queasy inside to be here, in the same hotel, on the opposite side of the wall from her. Good queasy.

No, bad queasy. Bad if he was going to concentrate on what the hell he was doing. Bad if he was going to keep his wits about him.

He stood up straight at the sound of boots in the hallway. Cleveland's boots? It was about time for him to take off for the saloon and the siren call of those pasteboards.

He crossed to the door and gently cracked it open. A figure, blond under the hat and fairly tall, was just turning the corner to go down the stairs. Fargo only caught a glimpse of him, but he was pretty damned sure he'd just seen Cleveland.

He figured he had about an hour.

He waited for a few minutes, giving Cleveland a

chance to get downstairs and trade pleasantries with the desk clerk. When Cleveland didn't come racing back up, Fargo was pretty certain that the desk clerk hadn't reported his presence. But still, he gave Cleveland enough time to leave the hotel and walk down the street, to the old Blue Goose Saloon.

You couldn't be too careful.

Especially now.

He let his room door swing back, swing open, and he stepped out into the hall, prepared to find just about anything in her room. But mostly, he was ready to find her bound and gagged, and looking toward him for help and succor.

He had plenty of each to give her.

Marga latched the door behind Cort Cleveland, then curled up on the bed with her book. Usually, she curled up with a mirror, but today she was feeling very pretty without one.

After all, they were almost there, almost to her goal. Lopez was only two days' ride from Chimney Ridge, and Chimney Ridge was where Mr. Clive Logan was waiting for her.

She closed her eyes and hugged herself. Logan represented freedom, freedom from her silly sister and socially concerned brother-in-law, freedom from people following her around night and day. Lower-caliber press people, that is, and those that informed her brother-in-law of her every step, her every move.

However, she didn't mind being followed by admirers.

Once, a man had followed her all day, just to ask the favor of touching her hem.

She smiled.

Someone rapped on the door.

She jerked her head toward it. It couldn't be the management. They'd made no noise. Yet.

Then who in the world?

"Marga?" said a low voice. An interesting voice. A voice filled with potential heat, she thought. But who on earth would know she was here? Who would know her name?

Girding her loins, she answered, "Who's out there? Who are you and what do you want?" She kept her tone cool, though. She didn't want to antagonize this stranger—until and unless it pleased her.

"Marga? I'm here to help you," whispered the voice.

Help her? Why would she need help?

"You are gallant, sir, but I need no assistance," she replied. The only one that could have possibly sent him was Madrid, her brother-in-law. The cur. He was here to drag her back to her sister's home!

"Let me in," the voice said, a bit louder now, more insistent. "Open the door, or I'll have the desk clerk do it."

"Damn!" she muttered under her breath, and got up, the bedsprings squeaking. She crossed to the door, but not before she opened her bag and took out a derringer, which she held behind her back.

"Marga?" the strange man said again. "Is he holding you against your will? *Can* you open the door? Are you all right?"

She unlatched the door and let it swing in, just a bit. "No one is holding me against my will, sir," she said, taking him in.

He was luscious—no other word for it. He was tall and lean, dressed in the manner of an Indian scout— all in fringed buckskins—and he had a sandy, close-cropped beard and light, ethereal, sky-blue eyes. There was something about the way he stood there— confident, yet concerned—that was very enticing.

Unconsciously, she licked her lips.

Come into my parlor, said the spider to the fly . . .

"Why did you come here, looking for me?" she purred.

52

The man in the hall asked, "May I come in?"

"But that is uncalled for," she said, smiling an unspoken invitation, despite her words. "After all, how would it look?"

The eyebrow of the man in the hall ticked once, and then, without warning, he reached out, quick as a cat, and grabbed her wrist. Before she knew it, he had pulled her out into the hall and was striding down it.

"Señor!" she yelped before she gathered herself. "This is reprehensible!" She wasn't frightened. She was only filled with umbrage and righteous indignation.

He didn't answer. He only continued to drag her into the next room, where he locked the door behind them.

She then remembered the derringer in her hand, and raised it. "If you do not let me out this second, sir, I shall be forced to shoot you."

He cocked his head at her, shaking it slightly. Then, more swiftly than the eye could see, he lashed out with his hand and knocked away the derringer. It hit the wall and dropped behind the dresser.

"I shall scream!" she shouted with a stamp of her foot.

"No, you won't," he said calmly. "You'll sit down. Please." He gestured toward the room's only chair.

Grudgingly, she sat. "Well?" she demanded, holding her hand—newly relieved of its derringer—to her breast. "What is it that you want?"

7

Fargo sat down on the bed, opposite her. God, she was a pistol, wasn't she? But he had to admit he'd never seen a better-looking pistol in all his born days. Her photograph hadn't half done her justice.

You had to see her in the flesh—in the light, in bright living color—for that.

Her eyes were a light violet. He'd never seen eyes that color before, and that was all he could think of— violets. They danced with reflected light and unexpected, sultry color. Her brows were dark, delicate, and perfectly arched, and her nose was flawless. Not a bump, not a hump, not the tiniest flaw. Just slim and straight and perfect.

And her mouth?

If he'd been a poet, he could have written a sonnet—no, a string of them—about her lips and the perfection of her teeth. Like pearls, they were, small and straight and even and white.

And her body?

That was just as magnificent. She was slim, but not too slim. Her bosom was full and high and round, her waist tiny, her hips softly belled and beckoning. Fargo found himself mentally undressing her, finding the flesh beneath that deep blue traveling dress, when he reeled himself back to shore.

With difficulty.

Finally, he said, "Marga, my name's Fargo. Skye Fargo. Your brother-in-law asked me to find you."

She closed her eyes—in disgust, Fargo thought.

Granted, it was an odd reaction, but then, he didn't know the history between the two of them. Maybe she ran off every five seconds. Maybe Madrid was always bringing her back from places she didn't wish to be brought back *from*.

She had no bruises, no signs of being swept away by a kidnapper or any kind of villain, really. Actually, Fargo himself seemed to have distressed her more than anything else.

"Diego!" she spat at last. "Again? Why can't he learn to mind his own business! This is America! I was born here! It is not Spain, not Mexico, and I don't need a baby-sitter! I do not need a *dueña*! I am a modern woman and I can take care of myself. Do you hear me?"

Fargo thought that there was something to that old saw about some women being prettier when they were mad. He hadn't seen her anything *but* mad so far, but he couldn't imagine anything more beautiful.

"Marga," he said, in a tone so gentle that even he hardly recognized it, "Madrid was just worried about you—that's all. Now, why don't you come on home with me, and you and he can—"

She rocketed to her feet and stamped her shoe on the floor, hard. "No!" she said sharply, her arms crossed firmly, her nose lifted. "I will not!"

Now, that put him a little on edge. Made him angry, in fact. He'd been a little rough on her, dragging her from her room and in here like that, but it was only because he figured that time was of the essence. He'd thought she was being held against her will and beaten silly by Cleveland, after all. Why else had he pushed the Ovaro—and himself—so hard?

But now?

He snapped, "How can you be hooked up with this huckster, Cort Cleveland? Are you helping him run his cons? A girl like you, with all the looks and money in the world!"

She tilted her head, like a beautiful and exotic bird. "I am most assuredly not helping him run any 'cons,' " she said, as if the word were unknown to her. "He is taking me somewhere. Somewhere I most certainly wish to go."

"And that would be?"

"None of your business!"

Spoiled brat. All right, he'd admit it. She was spoiled rotten. But still, her beauty saved her.

He said, in a more patient tone, "Marga, if you really want to be someplace specific, at least let me take you there."

He couldn't believe he had said that, but there it was.

Marge seemed to soften just a little.

She raised one perfect brow and asked, "You would do this for me? Who are you, again?"

He repeated, "Fargo. Skye Fargo."

Her eyes narrowed, but not in a bad way. It was as if she were concentrating, trying to place him.

She asked, "Fargo? You are the Fargo my brother-in-law speaks about?"

"Probably." He didn't figure there was another Fargo running around out here. Anyway, one that Madrid would speak of.

"The man of legend?"

He wasn't used to thinking of himself that way, but he liked the way that Marga asked it, and said, "Reckon I am."

"All right," she said, her face suddenly blooming into a smile that practically blinded him. "I shall accompany you, instead."

That this had been a little too easy only rapped very softly at the back of Fargo's brain, so softly that he paid it no mind. He was too smitten and too drunk on her presence to think clearly. And by God, he wanted to see her naked in the worst possible way!

Then he thought badly of himself for wanting to rip the clothing off such a proud creature.

But not all that badly.

Somehow, he managed to bring himself back down to earth again, and said, "This Cleveland. Will he be a problem?"

She arched a brow and sent him a conspiratorial look. "Not for the great Skye Fargo."

The flattery, coming from such an unearthly creature, nearly cut the legs out from under him. But he retained enough of his senses to ask, "Let's put 'the great Skye Fargo' aside for a minute. How's he likely to react? With bullets?"

Amazingly, she laughed. It was like music, and suddenly Fargo was imagining her standing there without a stitch on.

He shook his head to clear it. Dear God, this was going to be a whole lot more difficult than he had thought. He'd never had such an extreme reaction to a woman before. He was like a kid, he thought angrily, a clumsy sixteen-year-old kid with pimples, madly and secretly in love with the prettiest girl in town.

Except he wasn't a kid anymore, and Marga was worlds past pretty.

"He will not use his pistols," she said, still chuckling. "He is too much the coward to act alone."

He motioned her back into the chair, with a wave of his hand, and thankfully, she sat down again without a word of complaint. He wanted her on the same eye level as he was. And frankly, he couldn't stand up without being embarrassed.

"Where is it that you want to go?" he asked.

"Chimney Ridge." She said the words straight out, with no hesitation. "It was where Mr. Cleveland was taking me."

In exchange for what? he almost asked, but didn't. He didn't want to hear her say what he knew she would. And if she lied, and denied it, he didn't want to hear that, either.

"Why?" he asked instead.

Haughtily, she lifted her chin and stared down her beautiful nose at him. "That, sir, is none of your business."

And Fargo, despite himself, despite everything he knew to be right or sound or even sensible, stared into those pale violet, dark-lashed eyes, and said, "All right, Marga. I'll take you."

Owen Thurst and Red Neal, camped about twelve miles away from town, sat silently on opposite sides of their fire. Owen was speculating on what Fargo's face would look like at the moment of death.

The Lord only knows what Red was thinking about. He sat there, mindlessly chewing on his stewed ham and beans like a cow with its cud. As blank as a tree trunk, he stared out toward the stars.

Owen let out a snort. "How can anybody look so stupid?" he muttered, and Red looked over.

"You say somethin', Owen?"

Owen scooped up his plate and fork, and stood up. "I said, how can any man take so long to eat his supper." He walked over a few feet, then squatted down and began to rub his plate with a handful of sand.

He had slipped up, there, but it looked like he'd made a good save. Red said, "Oh," and returned to gazing up at nothing and slowly chewing.

One thing you had to say about Red, Owen thought, was that he sure made Owen feel, well, smart. It was certainly a different feeling than the one he got from a lot of those highfalutin fellows he met in the towns and villages they'd been through.

Fargo—now, there was a man who busted his butt!

Made him feel like he was as dumb as a rock, Fargo did. Always saying stuff that Owen didn't understand right off, if ever.

A man like that just plain shouldn't be allowed to live.

And pretty soon, Owen would take care of that—yes, sir. Pretty soon, Mr. Smart-Ass Fargo wouldn't be around to be so goddamned smart, to grab a man right out of his bedroll and turn him in to the law. Even when that man got his own self out of jail—by craft! by cunning!—Fargo had to come along and shoot him in his leg, by Christ! And then haul him in!

It was an embarrassment that Owen just couldn't get over. He had something of a reputation to live up to, after all. Hadn't that fellow up in Wyoming heard of him? He'd said that he had! And that kid, that kid who worked at the mercantile over in Bristol. He'd said he'd heard of Owen Thurst, too.

There. He had himself a reputation, all right. And that horse's backside, Fargo, just kept on going around and besmirching it. Making him look bad.

Well, this was going to be Fargo's very last chance, all right, and he wasn't going to live through it.

Now, Owen hadn't exactly figured out the logistics of the killing. He just had some sort of general idea of Red, stepping out with his gun—with Owen right behind him, of course—and shooting Fargo dead.

He supposed he ought to have a plan, except how was he to know where they'd catch up to the son of a bitch? Why, it might be in a town, with lots of pesky witnesses around, or it might be on the open plain. Or anyplace in between.

At last, the plate rubbed clean, he stood up, picking off the a few straggling grains of sand with a forefinger. "Red?" he said. "I been thinkin'."

There. Now that sounded important, didn't it?

Red apparently thought so, for he snapped to attention. Well, it was as snappy as Red got, anyhow. He even slopped a few beans off his plate when he turned toward Owen.

"What, Owen? What you been thinkin' about?"

"Been cogitatin' on it, Red," Owen said, in a tone that he hoped was profound. "I figure we shouldn't try to do nothin' in a town. There's too many people in towns. Somebody could see, and then they'd tell, and then we'd both go to jail."

Red nodded in agreement. "That's right smart, Owen. Long time ago, my daddy told me the same thing. 'Don't have no witnesses if there's a shootin',' he told me. 'Or a stabbin.' "

Annoyed that somebody had beaten him to this sage advice, Owen went on as if Red hadn't spoken. "What we do is wait until he gets alone, off by his lonesome, out on the desert or mountains or somethin'."

They were halfway between the low desert and the mountains at the moment, and Owen couldn't be sure which way Fargo would go next. But he figured to cover all his bases.

He added, "That's the time we take him, Red. That's the time I'm gonna signal you."

Eagerly, Red asked, "What signal, Owen? You gonna make a call like a hooty owl or somethin'?"

Owen's lips tightened, but he made them relax. He said, "No, Red, I'll just tell you. All right?"

"That's fine!" Red exclaimed. "Better than fine! 'Cause you could make a hooty owl call, you know, accidental like. This here Fargo . . . I'll be takin' out a real thorn in your side, won't I, Owen?"

"Yup. You sure will, Red."

Red smiled, the dumb son of a bitch. Then he said, "I sorta wish you'd do the hooty owl, though, Owen. I like that."

Owen sighed, and returned his cleaned plate to his saddlebags. "Maybe next time, Red."

* * *

Back in Lopez, down the street from the hotel where he had left Marga, Cort Cleveland was having a poor stay at the saloon, and at the poker table.

He was down fifteen dollars and seventy-five cents so far, and it didn't look like his luck was turning up. A deuce of clubs, a king of hearts; and the five, six, and eight of diamonds. Once again, he'd tried to fill an inside straight and he'd come up with exactly squat.

He had to stop doing this.

But then, that's what he'd been telling himself for almost a year, now.

Stop gambling.

Stop throwing your damned money away.

After all, he was supposed to be smart. He made his living on other people's stupidity. But lately, he'd been the one who was stupid. A real sucker—that was him.

He didn't listen to himself very well, but at least, lately, he'd been able to hold it down a good bit. One hour a night—that was it. He checked his pocket watch—or the wall clock if they had one—when he sat down, and the hand that he was playing, when an hour passed by, was his last hand of the night.

Nobody got mad at him. Nobody could.

Why, he told them, right when he sat down, that he was only playing an hour, win or lose. Usually, it was a loss. But sometimes it was a win. He clung to those memories—and the accompanying feelings—like a drowning man clings desperately to any flotsam he can find.

But by damn, it felt good to win! Like nothing else! Except maybe Marga.

But he was beginning to tire of Marga—when he wasn't near her, that is. Just lately, he was beginning to wonder what in the world had possessed him to help her with this lunatic plan.

Whatever it was.

She was sure awfully closemouthed, he thought.

You'd figure a girl like that wouldn't have a brain in her head. She wouldn't have had to grow one, to feed it or nurture it, with her being born so knock-down-drag-out pretty and all. He didn't think he'd ever seen another female top her in looks.

No, he was sure of it. No one else even came close. And she was a whole lot smarter than he'd suspected. She'd have to be, to con a confidence man into this . . . whatever it was.

Why, the first time he'd seen her, he'd been thunderstruck, and that was putting it mildly. He'd even walked out on that cozy deal he'd set up with Walters and Ortega, just to do what she wanted, take her where she wished, do her bidding.

He would have done anything for her.

Even died.

But as of late, his initial intoxication was wearing thin. What with the arguing—all right, downright fighting—and her throwing breakables and her demands, he was just about at the end of his rope with Her Royal Highness.

And he had a feeling—no, he was sure of it—that if he took her where she wanted to go, she'd disappear like his beer mug's wet ring, slowly evaporating, vanishing from the table top.

Except she'd go a whole lot quicker.

'Course, maybe that wasn't such a bad thing . . .

He checked his pocket watch. He still had fifteen minutes to play. Maybe his luck would turn in the next hand.

He said, "I'm folding on this one, boys." He laid his hand face down on the table, and waited for the next deal.

8

Marga arched a brow. He would take her there?

Well, naturally. Why wouldn't he? Fargo was a man, after all.

And besides, she was growing weary of Cort. If she had known that he was so obstreperous—not to mention his being such a poor lover—she would have picked another escort. After all a lady couldn't exactly travel alone across country. Cleveland just happened to be there, and just happened to be going her way, so to speak . . .

And he was handsome, in a faintly devious sort of way. It had held a certain appeal at the time.

But that time was long since over, she decided. This Fargo was far superior in every way. His clothing might be a little quaint, but it only added to the attraction. And then there were his eyes. So clear! She would have liked to fall into them, become lost in them.

She had not had a man such as this before. She had a strong feeling she would enjoy him.

She said, "You will take me there? Where I wish to go?"

Fargo didn't hesitate. "Yes," he said.

"Very well," she replied. "I will go with you. But first I must talk with Cort. He will be angry."

"Which means?" Fargo asked, his features knotted.

"Which means that he will be upset," she said. "But everything will be all right." She stroked and straightened her skirts. "I do not believe he'll put up too much of a fuss."

Fargo stared at her quizzically, and she stared back. His eyes, yes, those eyes! And beautiful hands, so strong, yet graceful, for a man. Suddenly, she wished she could enjoy him right now, without inhibition, and without the chance that Cort would return.

But he had been gone nearly an hour, and would soon be back.

"Why don't I believe you?" Fargo asked.

This completely stumped her. Why on earth would Fargo question her? Why would any man do so? Any man in his right mind, that is.

She lifted a brow and asked, "I beg your pardon? Do you doubt me?"

Fargo nodded. "I doubt Cort Cleveland's going to be so grand about you skipping out on him."

Her skin suddenly felt hot. "I do not 'skip out,' as you so crudely put it, sir!"

"Put it any way you want, Marga."

She rose to her feet and gave her foot a stomp. Crossing her arms, she announced, "Then I will not go with you. You are rude, sir! I will not be treated in this fashion by any man! And do not address me by my Christian name, if you please."

Fargo got to his feet, too. He towered over her. He looked down, scowling, and said, "Yes, you will, Marga. And I'd address you as 'Miss Something-or-other,' but Madrid didn't think to supply me with your last name."

He thumbed back his hat and leaned against the bureau. "See, I've been chasin' your tail all over hell and gone, and I'm not leaving without you. I can take you where you want to go, or I can toss you in a steamer trunk and ship you back to Madrid and his wife. Either one's fine with me. But I'm not letting you take one more step with Cleveland!"

This last part was almost a roar, and Marga blinked, enraged but stunned. And then her anger suddenly took a different turn.

This man had spirit. Not false bravado, like Cort Cleveland, but true spirit. He would not be one to scrap over details. He would only fight for what he thought was right and for the best.

Oddly enough, this pleased her, and in more ways than one. Between her legs, a warm, familiar fire kindled brightly.

A smile crept over her lips. "You have no manners, Fargo. You are rude. But I shall go with you. My way, not yours. I travel to the west, not the east and my brother-in-law."

Fargo let out a short, sharp breath through his nostrils. He was as ready for love as she was: she knew it, she felt it.

She was just about to take a step closer to him when Cort burst in from the hall, threw open the door, and stood there, panting with rage. His hands were balled into fists; his breath came hard. Anger and betrayal painted his face a deep red.

She turned to him.

"Hello, Cort darling," she purred.

Fargo's trigger finger itched, but he didn't draw. He merely stood his ground and waited. Besides, Cleveland looked to be unarmed.

He also appeared to be flummoxed.

Cleveland stood there in the doorway, sputtering, not making any sense, until finally, he burst out, "What's going on here, Marga? Who's this stranger, and why are you in his room?"

Marga went to Cleveland, and part of Fargo wanted

to reach out and pull her back. But he didn't. He watched as Marga took Cleveland's arm and reached up to stroke his face.

"Now, my pet," she purred, "don't be angry. This is Mr. Fargo, and he has just alleviated you of the responsibility of taking me farther west. Now you can gamble to your heart's content, my dear Cort, and get back to your life. And you won't have to give me another thought."

Cort hadn't looked at her since pushing in the door. He glared at Fargo. "I don't want to gamble," he growled in a low voice.

"Yes, you do, pet," she cooed. She reached up and took his jaw in her hand, gently turned it until he was looking at her, and then added, "Dearest, you know how we bicker. I know you've been waiting for the moment when you could drop me off, but you were too gallant to say anything. My knight, my handsome white knight, your job is finished."

She stood on her tiptoes and kissed him, and Fargo felt jealousy surge through him like a raging river. Jealousy? Just moments ago, he'd recovered himself enough so that he was threatening to toss her in a truck and ship her back to Madrid and Rosa!

How could the mere presence of her lover—her former lover, hopefully—bring out this strong a response in him? He didn't know. It was something beyond reason, something beyond conscious thought. Something that he barely had under control.

But nobody was looking at him. Neither of them was aware, it seemed, of his presence.

Cort looked deep into Marga's eyes. "But I love you," he said, and Fargo felt that flooding river rise even higher.

"But you don't, my darling," Marga said softly. "You are in love with the idea of me. I shall remember your kindness always, Cort. I shall always remember you fondly. But you must let me go on with Mr. Fargo. He will deliver me safely into Logan's hands."

Cleveland's breath came in short little rasps, and Fargo could tell he was at the breaking point. He knew that he was.

And who the hell was Logan, anyway? Was she setting Fargo up for the same scene she was playing out with Cleveland?

Well, of course she was! He came back into himself with a start.

Don't be an idiot, Fargo. She's business, plain and simple.

Except he knew she was neither plain nor simple. She wasn't like anyone else, and this job he'd taken on was like no other.

And why the hell had he told her he'd take her farther away from Madrid? Madrid had hired him, after all. Not her. She should be no more than a job to him, no less.

But she was much, much more—inexplicably, after he'd known her for only a few minutes, she was.

"Won't you let me go, dear Cort, sweet Cort?" Marga was cooing. She kissed his lips.

It had better be for the goddamn last time, Fargo thought, his hands balling into fists. *He touches her again, I'll kill him.*

Oddly enough, though, Cort whispered, "Anything you wish, my darling." And then he took a step back, into the hall, out of her embrace. He had himself under control now, it appeared. He stood straight, almost stiffly, and added, "Do what you wish."

"I wish to get my things," Marga said, and smiled.

"Fine, then. I wish you God's speed." Cort took another step back and ushered her out and down the hall.

"Don't worry, Fargo," she called back over her shoulder. "I'll return in a few moments."

And they were gone.

Fargo sat down hard on the bed and shook his head like a dog fresh from the waters of the Big Muddy.

What the hell had just happened?

"And I'll have the roast lamb," Marga was saying to the waiter.

It turned out that this little hamlet had a passable restaurant, and Fargo had decided that the best place to take Marga right at the moment was, well, someplace besides his hotel room.

He'd guessed that perhaps he'd think better there. It wasn't making much difference, though. He'd followed her down from the hotel like a lovesick puppy, and he knew it. Hell, everybody who'd seen them walking down the street knew it, too.

She leaned across the table and whispered, "I would ask for the wine list, but I didn't want to embarrass them. I doubt very much if they have any wine. Of decent vintage, anyway." She played with her water glass.

She might as well have mentioned that they didn't have any ivory-handled button hooks or solid silver fish forks, either.

"This is nice," she continued. "Getting out, I mean. Cort brought my meals to my room."

"Why?" Fargo managed.

"Well . . ." She shrugged. "There was a nasty bit of business a few towns back. Someone in the café. Cort didn't want it to happen again."

She didn't explain, but Fargo knew what had probably happened. Her beauty had reeled in a man without self-restraint—or without manners—who had made a pass at her. Right under Cort's nose. As it was, a quick glance around the dining room told him that every man in the place was staring at her.

Fargo understood immediately, all right, now that he was in Cort Cleveland's boots.

He was still befuddled by the way Cort had left them. He gave up so easily! Fargo wondered how the hell he'd managed. And why?

Cort had been madder than a bag full of badgers when she first told him, and Fargo had expected a fight. And he'd been willing. Guns, knives, fists—it didn't matter. Where Marga was involved, he seemed to lose all sense of self-restraint.

All sense of self-preservation, too.

But Cort hadn't made a move on him. He hadn't made a move, period. He'd just walked back to their room with her, helped her get her things together, then carried her bag to Fargo's room.

All without a word.

Fargo didn't know Cort Cleveland from a hole in the ground, but he knew his type. Silence—and giving in so easily—wasn't the way that type operated. Not that he figured Cort would come gunning for him: no, he imagined Cort might try something devious, in keeping with his profession.

Still, he was concerned enough that at least some of his instincts were still functioning. He'd ushered Marga to a table at the rear of the room and sat with his back against the wall, so that he had a full view of the door, the front windows, and the street outside.

And all those male patrons, staring.

And what he saw, too, as he listened to Marga talk and waited for their meal to arrive, was Cort Cleveland himself, mounted on the bay and riding out of town.

Wordlessly, he pointed, and Marga turned, saw Cort ride past the window, then swiveled back toward Fargo. She shrugged. "He is gone."

Fargo was still staring out the window. "Where'll he go off to?"

If we're lucky, he won't go our way, he thought.

"I don't know," she replied with a shrug, as if Cort were a stranger, someone she had only just met, and about whom she couldn't have cared less.

Fargo had one of those interior jolts again, a jolt that brought him back to his senses. At least, halfway. "He won't follow us?" he asked leerily.

"Oh, no," she said, tearing a tiny piece off of her roll and holding it near her mouth. "He'll probably go back to New Mexico. I believe he had some business there that I interrupted."

True, Cort was headed out of town the way he'd come. That didn't mean he couldn't circle around, though. *But then,* Fargo thought, *maybe Marga has pushed me over the edge. Maybe I've lost all my senses, including the one for self-preservation.*

He was aware that she affected him to the point that he could barely think when she was around. Maybe he was giving Cleveland too much credence. Maybe he was just a second-rate con artist without the guts to keep his hands on Marga. Maybe he was just slinking out of town.

Then again, maybe Fargo's brain had totally gone to mush.

He didn't know what to think anymore.

The waiter brought their meal, and they refrained from speaking until Fargo pushed his plate away. Marga was just picking at hers.

She said, "Those potatoes were unspeakable."

He'd been thinking that the less he saw of Marga, the better off he'd be. He needed to straighten himself out before morning. And he'd decided to get her a room of her own, once they got back to the hotel. But now he wouldn't have to, would he? She could sleep in Cleveland's unused bed, and save him the expense.

And besides, he didn't see that there had been anything wrong with the potatoes. He'd eaten every last crunchy bit of his.

Without a preamble, he stood up. "Let's get back to the hotel," he said.

Rising, she tipped her head and smiled slyly. Those

violet eyes danced mischievously. "You're the anxious one, aren't you?"

"No," Fargo lied, as he dropped his napkin on the table. "I just want to get an early start in the morning."

He lay in his hotel bed, staring angrily at the ceiling. He was at war with himself, and couldn't seem to call a truce long enough to get any shut-eye at all. First, he was mad because he knew damn well that Marga was going to take him for a ride. Hell, she'd already started! He was mad at himself for being a fool, and knowing it, and letting it happen!

And then he was angry with himself for not taking advantage of the situation. She was over there, on the other side of the wall, just the thickness of a couple of wall boards between them. And what if people thought he was a fool, if even *he* thought he was a fool? They weren't the ones who had the pleasure of being under Marga's spell, were they?

And then he'd start all over again.

And buzzing behind all this self-recrimination were far too many unanswered questions. Why had Cort Cleveland given in so easily? Who the hell was this Logan she was meeting, and why was she meeting him?

She hadn't brought along much, just the contents of that one small bag. She'd left behind the world as she knew it. She'd left money, and everything it could buy: fancy clothes, jewelry, that grand hotel suite of Madrid's (and his and his wife's far grander home on the ranch), servants, and goddamn wine lists. Her reasons for leaving, for running off, had to be important.

He just wished he knew what they were.

He wished he'd never met her.

He wished he'd invited her into his room.

He wished he were back in New Mexico, drunk in

a cantina somewhere and in the fleshy arms of a nice, benign, soiled dove.

He wished that Margae were here with him now, naked and in his arms, with her violet eyes and her hair all undone . . .

Fargo, he told himself, *you are a jackass.*

9

Cort Cleveland picked his way along the trail. The clouds had moved again to cover the moon, and he was in trouble.

He asked himself why he was out here on this stupid horse when he should have been traveling by stage at the very least, and the answer came back: Marga.

He asked himself why he had put himself in the middle of Apache country, all alone; why he was seventy miles from any place containing remotely civilized people, or a railroad, or even men barely worth fleecing, and again, the answer came back: Marga.

But still . . .

His horse stumbled.

He nearly went off over its head and hung there, clinging to its mane with his fists knotted full of hair, and muttering to himself about how all men are idiots—and he certainly qualified—and how he was going to get a concussion in the middle of nowhere and possibly die, all because of a woman.

A stupid woman.

No, not just a woman. Not just any woman.

Marga.

He righted himself with some difficulty, took a breath, and then dismounted, as only a man who has spent nearly the whole of his life at card tables—and in train depots and bedrooms and back rooms—can dismount: badly. But he got off and slowly led the horse off the side of what passed for a road, stumbling over his own feet and the horse's.

It was too dark to see, but he managed to loosen the horse's girth and sit down on the ground by nothing more than feel. That was one thing that his life and travails had taught him, at least. To feel his way through the dark.

It was a small comfort. Even since he'd left town with his tail between his legs, he'd been having second thoughts: minor at first, but growing stronger all the time.

Why should he, the great—all right, the pretty good— Cort Cleveland step aside for the likes of Fargo?

This Fargo was nothing more than a two-bit gunman! Why, the man couldn't even afford real clothes. He had to shoot them!

Sure, he'd been floored when he heard Fargo's name. It had put him into a state of shock, actually. Just standing in the same room with Fargo had made Cleveland's knees a little shaky. He was surprised that they hadn't given out an audible knock.

He'd heard the stories, of course. At least, he'd heard enough that even if Marga hadn't said the man's name, he would have known Fargo on sight. Well, eventually.

That was one thing about the con game. You heard all the stories faster, all the interesting details about famous men, and who was good with a con or a gun and who wasn't. More like who was dead and who wasn't.

Same thing.

He reached into his pocket, pulled out his cigar case, and fumbled for a match. But he noticed that when he popped the match into flame and held it to the slim Havana, his fingers were shaking. Still.

Damn!

*   *   *

74

Marga sat in the deep armchair, her feel curled beneath her. She stared out the window and wondered again how on earth Fargo could have sent her from his room. Why, it was unheard of!

Men would die for even a whisper of a *hint* of a chance with her!

And Fargo had sent her away?

It was madness.

At first, when she had come back to her room, she had ripped off her dress and donned her nightgown: a flimsy wisp of rose-colored silk that skittered over her curves as if it wasn't there at all.

But then, with her hand on the door's latch, she'd had second thoughts.

She—the wondrously beautiful and wildly talented Margarita Elizabeth Trentwell-Oberon—beg?

No!

It was unheard of!

So she'd slumped down in this chair to pout, and had been staring out into the bottomless black of the vacant street ever since.

It made her angry—that's what it did. No, it made her feel betrayed and hurt.

No, insulted.

No . . .

Actually, she wasn't sure how it made her feel. After all, nothing remotely like it had ever happened to her before. But however she was feeling, she didn't like it.

Fumbling in the dark, she reached for her watch pin, then angled it so that it caught the feeble light of the moon. Squinting, she stared at it until it came into soft focus.

Almost midnight.

She slumped back. Almost midnight, and he had not yet come rapping at her door. Well, she'd be damned if she would go and knock at his!

Who the hell did he think he was, anyway? she

thought with a snort. Why, only last month, the Spanish ambassador had clamored for her!

Did Fargo think he was better than the Spanish ambassador?

She rose from her chair and felt her way, finally, to the bed. She settled back, thinking that he would never have her if he was so callous, so stupid, so pigheaded as to turn down such a grand and gracious offer. He could take her on to Chimney Ridge, and Logan.

But that, she swore to herself, was all.

Period.

Cort Cleveland awoke the next morning in exactly the same place where he'd sat down the night before. Other than falling backward from a sitting position to his current one—flat out on the ground—he hadn't moved a muscle.

His horse still stood patiently nearby, and the dawn was just breaking, sending the first slivers of pink and orange and purple light out from the eastern horizon into a fading charcoal night.

He sat up, wincing at cramped muscles and angry bones not accustomed to the insult of sleeping on the ground, and he creakily got to his feet.

"All right, all right, dammit," he muttered to his horse when it nickered at him and nudged his sore back with its nose. "I've got some grain and water somewhere here . . ."

Cursing the horse, Fargo, Marga, and the fickle condition of women everywhere, he began to dig through his saddlebags.

Fargo was already up. At the basin on the dresser, he poured out water and splashed it over his face. He felt better, but not much.

He had not slept soundly.

Who could, knowing that Marga—he had to remember to ask her last name!—was on the other side of the wall? Who in his right mind, anyway . . . ?

He gave himself another mental kick, something he'd been doing off and on all through the night. These next few days were going to be hell. Pure hell.

He dressed, let himself out of his room, and listened at her door.

Nothing.

He debated whether to wake her or not, then decided against it. He didn't suppose she was used to getting up at five in the morning, and he wasn't going to give her another reason to hate him.

She had enough of those already.

And she'd sure be mad enough when he told her. Mad? That was being nice about it. He'd decided to haul her back to New Mexico, instead of where she wanted to go. After all, Diego Madrid was paying, and Madrid wanted her back, whether she liked it or not.

He just hoped to hell that once she was standing there in front of him, he wouldn't weaken again. Admittedly, she had an effect on him like no other woman.

Hell's bells—if she'd asked him to dance naked in the street last night, he probably would have done it with a grin on his face!

He was a fool of the first water—there was no doubt about it.

As he made his way downstairs and then walked out into the street, he felt her hold on him—or whatever it was, dammit—lessen a little. And when he walked down the street toward the livery, he felt his burden lighten even more.

Yes, sir, he told himself, he'd take her back to New Mexico—that was it. Back to the town of Quake and Madrid's hotel suite and her ever-loving sister, the ice queen—that was where she was going, even if he had to hogtie and gag her.

He didn't understand why she'd run away in the

first place. As he arrived at the livery and began to brush down the Ovaro's glistening hide, he asked himself what purpose she could possibly have had.

Why on earth—if Cleveland meant nothing to her, a fact she'd pretty much proven by brushing him off with so little remorse—had she taken a chance on traveling through Apache territory? Particularly with somebody who wasn't equipped to protect her from Indians, bandidos, just plain bad men, or anything else untoward that she might run across in the wild country?

No matter how he turned it around in his head, it didn't stack up.

There had to be a reason. Where the hell was she going, and why?

No—correction: Where did she *want* to go?

Not that it mattered, he thought, moving around to the other side of the Ovaro. He wasn't taking her there, anyway. Not him.

He'd be damned if he'd let a woman wrap him around her finger like that.

When Marga awoke, light poured in from the window, and the street below was full of the sounds of buggies and hoofbeats and casual shouts. Groping on the night stand, she found her watch pin and raised it to sleepy eyes. Eight thirty.

She sank back down on her pillow and made a face. She supposed she'd best get up and get started. Fargo was likely as much of an early morning riser as Cleveland had been. She was not, though. Early, to her, meant any time before noon.

And will again soon, she told herself. The moment she got to Chimney Ridge, the moment she got to Mr. Clive Logan . . . Well, he would know how to treat a lady. A great lady!

Mr. Clive Logan was nothing like these thugs with

whom she had been forced to consort, simply to move a few miles across country.

Logan would be a man of refinement—she was certain of it. He would have to be, being in the business he had chosen, wouldn't he? Mr. Carlos Sweeney would hire no less.

She washed as best she could in the water from the bowl and pitcher, then dressed carefully, all the time reminding herself that she would not speak to Fargo any more than she had to.

He had insulted her honor—that's what—when he had sent her to her room last night. He had insulted her honor and her beauty and her importance.

Why, the man was no more than a glorified shootist! A backwoods murderer. Imagine—being famous for killing people!

The entire concept was barbaric. And Fargo? He was dirt under her shoe.

She opened the door of her room, only to find Fargo standing in the hallway. Startled, she stopped. And he seemed startled, too, even though he'd obviously been waiting for her. He stood up straighter. His Adam's apple bobbed once, then twice.

At last, he spoke. "Breakfast?" he said.

She nodded curtly, but felt her resolve melting. He was so handsome, with those cool eyes burning out of that handsome, tanned face like ice in summer, and that lean, hard body that she knew must be beneath the buckskins.

She could see his muscles flex and relax even as he stood erect and offered his arm.

A shiver went through her, but she managed to hide it from him. She hoped. She had her pride, after all, although it seemed to be fading by the second.

"That would be lovely, Mr. Fargo," she said, and took his arm. "Lead on."

10

All that resolve, thought Fargo, *down the well. So much for being stern with her.*

Not only was he taking her to Chimney Ridge, but he was doing it happily. At least, he'd agreed to it that way. And right at that moment, as they were riding through the brush, scaring up the occasional covey of quail or sending a jackrabbit bounding, she was humming contentedly to herself.

At least, he thought she was humming. To be honest, he couldn't be certain that it wasn't a bad case of indigestion until he turned and looked over at her, and saw she was smiling.

Oh, well. He could put up with a little off-key drone, ear-jarring as it was, just for the sake of looking at her. Christ, she was even more beautiful in the sunlight than she had been last night, if that were possible.

Of course, her good mood probably had a lot to do with the direction in which they were going. She'd been as perky as a pup since he promised to take her where she wanted to go. Of course, she still hadn't told him why she wanted to go there—or who this Logan was, either—but at least she'd told him her name.

Margarita Elizabeth Trentwell-Oberon. Now, wasn't that a dandy?

Of course, he felt bad about giving in so easily. He still couldn't nail down the exact reason, except that when she was around, he just couldn't seem to say no to her.

Hell, she didn't even have to ask! He just naturally did what she wanted.

In a way, it was pretty goddamn unnerving.

But at the moment, he wasn't wondering about that—he was thinking, instead, about what was going to happen once they got to Chimney Ridge.

He hadn't been there before. The town was too new, and had sprung up since he'd been through this part of the territory. He couldn't imagine there would be much of anything there, but Marga assured him that the railroad came through. It was a thriving community with a theater, she'd said.

And, of course, he'd believed her. Well, he believed that *she* believed. He knew damned well that the railroad hadn't come within two hundred miles of where they were right now.

And ahead?

There was nothing but desert. If you put enough of that under your horse's hooves, you'd get to California and eventually the Pacific Ocean, but that was it.

And he doubted that a few years was enough time to build a "thriving community," complete with a theater.

In these parts, a town would be lucky to have a traveling singer or a dancer come through once in a blue moon. The "theater" would most likely be the local saloon; the stage would probably be a couple of boards set up on two barrels; and the entertainment, whatever it was, would more than likely be punctuated by gunshots from a rowdy audience.

Fired directly at the entertainer, if he or she wasn't lucky. Or wasn't any good.

So much for a theater. And the railroad. He was afraid that Marga—his beautiful, enchanting, fabulous, damnable Marga—was going to be in for a letdown.

He wasn't the one who'd tell her, though—not a chance of it. Although he'd be first in line to comfort her when she found out. Right now he just wanted to keep her in a good mood for as long as possible. Life was a lot nicer that way.

Nicer, hell! Life was wonderful. And it would be past perfect if she'd just stop that damned humming.

Oh, well. Who was he to quibble?

As he slowly headed back east, Cort Cleveland heard hoofbeats approaching from around the bend. His first thought was *Indians!*—even though he had yet to see one—and he rode off the trail and toward cover before he realized what he was doing.

But halfway down to the few feeble trees, somebody with a deep, gravelly voice shouted, "Whoa up there, Mister!"

Somebody else shouted, "Hold it, buddy, or I'll shoot!"

And Cort Cleveland reined in, also before he realized it. He turned back toward the voices, knowing all the while that whether you were killed by wild Indians or white men in suits, you ended up just as dead. But he was unable to resist the possibility of putting off being shot in the back for at least a few minutes longer.

But they weren't white men in suits. They were white men in filthy clothes. They didn't look any too clean beneath them, either. One had flaming red hair and a few days of stubble covering his dull features, and the other was dark and had a slightly caved-in chest that made him appear, at first glance, a little like a hunchback. He didn't look to have shaved in a good week, either.

The redheaded one had his gun drawn, and it was aimed right at Cleveland's heart, which was beating wildly. He was a fool to ever have come this far west!

But Cleveland, ever the confidence man, turned on a big smile despite his better instincts. "Good morning, gents," he said, nodding at them in his friendliest fashion.

His toothy smile and good manners had gotten him out of a good deal of trouble before. Of course, he didn't figure that good manners went too far in convincing the unwashed, but he was certainly going to give it his best try.

After all, it seemed his life depended on it.

The red-headed one held the gun steady while the dark one with the sunken chest leaned over and muttered something to him in a low rumble.

Then the redheaded one said, "Your money or your life, Mister."

The dark-haired one rolled his eyes.

This put Cort Cleveland in a bit of a dilemma. He hadn't a dollar to his name. Marga had been footing the bill for their food and lodging, as well as that of their horses. He wondered if they'd just shoot him, as a matter of course, when he confessed that he was broke.

But he didn't have much choice. He said, "Gentlemen, I am truly sorry to disappoint you." He shrugged his shoulders. "I haven't a cent."

Actually, he had roughly twenty-seven cents, but the coins were in his sock and he didn't figure these two would look there. Unless they killed him first.

Of course, then it would be a moot point.

But the redheaded one wasn't going to be put off. He wiggled the muzzle of his gun and demanded, "Give over your purse or face the . . . the . . ."

"Consequences?" Cort asked helpfully.

"Yeah, those," barked the gunman.

All right, Cort thought. He began to see a feeble light at the end of the proverbial tunnel. *I see. I can handle this. I hope.*

"Gentlemen, gentlemen!" Cort began. "I'm terribly sorry, but I haven't a sou to my name. I only wish that I did. I was relieved of all my earthly possessions back in—"

"Can I shoot him, Owen?" the redheaded one asked his friend.

Cort swallowed, hard. He'd tried. He was about to open his mouth to try again, to spin them a bit of fiction about how he had been bilked at poker.

But then, before he could get started, the dark one, Owen, growled, "Save it for Fargo."

"Fargo?" Cort piped up. He couldn't help himself. "Did you mention Fargo? *The* Skye Fargo?"

Owen's features wrinkled. "What about it?"

"Do you . . . do you have business with him?" Cort asked carefully.

"What's it to you, tinhorn?" the redheaded one asked nastily. He appeared to be enjoying this far too much, Cort thought.

He also thought that they seemed too touchy about Fargo to want to shower him with gifts. It was much more likely that they wanted to shower him with fists and bullets, and perhaps a rock or two.

Cort took a chance and snapped, "That son of a bitch! I'd like to kill him!"

The nose of the redheaded one's gun dropped a few inches, and Owen leaned forward a tad.

"Why come?" asked Owen.

Cort told the truth for one of the few times in his life.

"He made off with my woman," he admitted with a touch of shame. The story was so good that if it hadn't been the truth, he probably would have made

84

it up. "That rat bastard," he added, and spat down into the weeds for good measure.

Owen waved his hand and said, "Put that Colt away, Red."

Red? Owen thought, with a little snort. *That figures.*

But he said, "Thank you, gentlemen," and bowed his head slightly. "I take it that you have had some trouble with this Fargo devil yourselves!"

Pump up the con, he thought. *Make yourself as foreign to their type as you possibly can. With one exception . . .*

"You're damned right, we have," Owen said with a snarl.

· "That's right!" echoed Red.

Owen asked, "Where'd you run into the bastard?"

Cort Cleveland poked a thumb up the road down which he'd come. "In Lopez," he said, and then shook his head in disgust. "Gentlemen, I am most distraught. I fear my darling Miss Marga will be much the worse for wear when I see her next. *If* I ever see her again."

He gave out a theatrical sigh. He said, "That Satan in disguise, Fargo, bamboozled her! A few soft words of sugar, and she was convinced to leave me. I tell you, he is a rogue of the first water! He deserves to die, and worse."

Red nodded, giving Cort the impression that every word he'd said had flown far over Red's head—with the possible exception of the part about Fargo deserving to die—but Owen Thurst seemed to have taken his point.

In fact, he seemed to have fallen for it—hook, line, and sinker.

Nodding, Owen said, "Fargo's a devil all right, Mister. He put me in jail two whole times and shot me up, to boot." He seemed to consider something, and then said, "You wanna come along?"

Cort looked shocked, or so he hoped. "Come along?" he asked. "With you?" He tried to appear as if he considered himself unworthy to travel with this road trash.

"We's gonna kill that Fargo dead," Red said gleefully.

"That's right," Owen echoed.

Cort appeared to consider this. At last, he said, "Then allow me to introduce myself, gentlemen, if we are going to be traveling companions. I'm Cort Cleveland, a wronged man."

Owen nodded. "Howdy, Cleveland. I'm Owen Thurst, and this here," he said, nodding at his sidekick, "is Red Neal. He's the best damn shot in the territory. Mayhap two territories."

Red beamed.

"Delighted, gentlemen," Cort said. "Delighted to make your acquaintances."

"So, how come you're named after a city, Mr. Cleveland?" Red asked.

Cort blinked.

"Don't pay him no mind," Owen said in unveiled disgust. He reined his horse up onto the road. "He's sort of squirrelly. How come you're goin' away when your woman's back to Lopez?"

Cort gave his horse a nudge with his heels, and joined Owen on the road. Red rode up behind him. He wasn't certain whether he liked that part—Red being behind him—or not, but right now wasn't the time to do anything about it.

With just the right touch of weary cowardice, Cort said, "I fear I am not up to outdrawing this fiend, Fargo, Mr. Thurst. Sadly, I know my limitations. Perhaps if I had assistance . . ."

Owen laughed. "Cleveland, you just got yourself some real willin' 'assistance.' Me and Red, here? We're goin' to kill that horse's backside. Kill him deader than shit. And we're lettin' you come along for the ride."

Cleveland opened his mouth, but before he could

speak, Red asked, "How come we're lettin' him do that, Owen?"

Owen rolled his eyes, then turned in his saddle. "Because," he shouted back, "it sounds like a good idea, Red."

"Oh," said Red, nodding. "Okay, then."

To a relieved Cort, Owen said, "You gotta pardon him. He don't know about things like this. You know, 'bout like-minded souls and all that."

"Ah," said Cort, who didn't understand, either, and hadn't been able to use any of the quickly-thought-up reasons why he should be allowed to accompany them. "I see," he said.

"Damn right," Owen said. "You're what you call . . . a man of the world. I could tell that just by lookin' at you."

Which is why you tried to hold me up, you idiot, Cort thought dryly.

"Ah," he said, again.

"They still in Lopez?" Red asked from the rear.

"No, Mr. Neal," Cort replied. "I believe not. But I know where they are going."

Owen slapped his thigh, and a cloud of dust rose from his britches. "See there, Red? I knowed he'd come in handy!"

Inwardly, Cort smiled smugly. "If there is any way in which I might be of assistance in achieving your goal—and mine—Mr. Thurst, I shall be more than happy to cooperate in any way possible. I, too, would be deliriously happy to see Mr. Fargo . . . —how do you westerners say it?"

He pretended to mentally grope and search for the words. "Dead in a ditch," he announced at last. "That's it."

Behind him, Red laughed, and Owen joined in.

"Yessir, Cleveland," Owen said, still chortling— though, Cort thought, a little too nastily—"you're gonna fit in just fine. Now, where'd you say they was headed?"

11

"All right, honey," Fargo said. "Let's stop and give the horses a breather."

It was midday. Fargo figured they'd make Chimney Ridge in about a day and a half, which would make for one night on the trail. One night for which he had very high hopes.

Mercifully, Marga had stopped humming quite a while ago. And right then, as she dismounted, with her fancy little backside swishing, Fargo was looking forward to the night that much more.

"And what are we having for luncheon?" she asked brightly. Those eyes were incredible.

Luncheon? He gave his head a shake. Hell, it wasn't like he had a tea set, a butler, and those little cucumber sandwiches in his saddlebags. And he suddenly felt as if he needed them to be, well, worthy.

He said, "Sorry, Marga. We're going to have to settle for boiled eggs and jerky." It was lousy fare, but it was the best he could do.

She made a face.

"I didn't exactly plan on . . ." he began lamely.

"It's all right, my dear Fargo," she said quickly, with a flutter of those sooty lashes. "It would be entertaining to—how do you say?—'rough it.'" She smiled.

It was enough for Fargo.

*   *   *

Perhaps I've been too harsh, Marga thought, as
Fargo watered the horses. The muscles of his back
and shoulders slithered like steel snakes beneath the
deer hide of his buckskins, and she hungrily licked
her lips.

Actually, she'd been thinking the same thing since
breakfast. Perhaps she'd been a little too strident in
her thinking about shutting him out, keeping him
away. Maybe she should give him a chance. He looked
so . . . inviting.

Definitely.

She rose from her perch atop a boulder, and
straightened her skirts carefully, purposefully. There
would only be one night before she passed from his
hands into Logan's. And she had the distinct feeling
that one night would not be enough.

This Fargo was, well, he was a *man*! She would take
advantage. If he'd have her, that is. She wasn't entirely
certain after last night, but she'd take a chance.

He was worth it.

Smoothing her hair even though it was perfect—as
usual—Marga softly walked toward his back. She
paused when she came within reach, took a breath,
and touched his shoulder.

It was as if a shock had passed between them, and
she jumped, feeling not only the spark, but a sudden,
greater gush of warmth between her legs.

"Fargo," she whispered. "Take me."

Fargo blinked at the shock of her, both literal and
figurative. But this time, he didn't hesitate. He took
her into his arms and kissed her long and deep, and
was gratified when he felt her melt into his embrace.
If she was offering, he was by God taking, and no
questions asked.

Fargo was a lot of things, but he wasn't a fool.

They ripped at each other's clothing, although he

had an easier time with her blue bodice than she did with his bucks; and her breasts, ripe and round and flawless, popped out into his waiting hands.

Quickly, he skinned out of his britches, took her to the ground, and lifted her skirts to the sound of her breathy and urgent "Hurry, my Fargo, hurry!"

Before he mounted her, she pulled him close and said, "I want you. I want you deep inside me, my darling." Her hand went to his member, and her touch was like fire as she guided him to her portal.

As if he needed help! Hell, the way he felt right now, he could have found her in the middle of a moonless night on a vast and open plain!

He slid into her, feeling the welcoming comfort of her inner walls, and she sighed happily, or perhaps in exaltation. He couldn't tell.

Her fingers toyed with the hair on the back of his neck while her free hand moved beneath his leather shirt, skimming over muscles, teasing flesh, then dropping to firmly grip his backside.

"Yes, Fargo, yes," she breathed. Her eyes were slitted, her parted lips were an open invitation. "Now, please."

He kissed her again, and then he began to move. She was a feast for the starving, a banquet, any way you looked at it. She moved beneath him as if they had been made for each other, meeting every thrust, every parry, urging him on with enthusiastic little moans and whispers and whimpers.

Her knees were at his sides, gripping him tightly outside while her internal muscles hugged him within. "Yes, Fargo! Yes!" she breathed, her beautiful face contorting with passion as she squirmed and writhed beneath him.

He didn't need the urging. In what seemed like no time at all, he felt the demanding tickle in his loins grow to a heady flame, surge wildly, and then suddenly kindle into a glorious conflagration that burned brighter and brighter and then . . .

He climaxed in a pure, luminescent, fantastically bright burst that emptied him of all the frustrations of the past day.

And which, for the moment, at least, left him levelheaded.

She had come to fruition, also, with a tiny, trembling, strangled scream. She now lay beneath him, panting and sated and looking, if it were possible, even more angelic, more comely, more sensuously beautiful.

He kissed her again, kissed her lips and her eyes and her temples, and she smiled slyly.

"Fargo, you are the best," she whispered. "The very best."

And you should know, he thought, then kicked himself mentally for having thought it.

Instead of speaking, he rolled off of her, then hooked his arm beneath her head, pillowing it. She sighed, and he stroked her cheek and played with her breasts, teasing idly at the nipples.

She was right up there, he thought, right up there with the best.

But the best what?

The best whores he'd ever been with, he realized. And for some odd reason, he, who had never held anything against a good whore in his life—except his pecker, that is—felt a bad taste come into his mouth.

It took him a moment to realize why. And then it hit him.

He'd been had.

But hell, he'd wanted to be, hadn't he? He'd wanted her in the worst possible way! There was no way around the truth of that.

But she had wanted him just as badly—just as she seemed to want everyone.

Badly.

Intensely.

She has a problem with men, Madrid had said.

And the problem was, Fargo knew, that she couldn't keep away from them. She'd likely bedded half the territory of New Mexico. The male half, anyway.

Madrid had been too kind. He'd barely skimmed the surface.

And Fargo felt something that he hadn't thought he could feel: used. As used as the cheapest whore in a barrel-and-plank saloon.

It was a completely new sensation for him, and he didn't quite know how to cope with it.

He sat up abruptly, pulling his arm from beneath her head.

"Ouch!" she yelped, when her head unceremoniously hit the hard ground. "What are you doing?"

He pulled on his britches, fixed her skirts, then gave her a hand up before he spoke. It took him that long to think of something to say.

And then it was only, "We'd better get moving, Marga."

She cocked her head, staring at him oddly. She seemed to be searching him for some clue as to why she was being treated with such . . . discourtesy, he supposed. He didn't mean to be discourteous. Or rude. Or insensitive.

He was just plain uncomfortable, and not exactly certain why.

He forced a smile and touched her cheek. "We can eat on the move, honey," he added, then cursed himself for not acting more the part of the lover, the lover who had just nailed down the finest piece of ass west of the Mississippi.

Am I going crazy? he asked himself, as he helped her to her horse.

And the puzzled look that rode her flawless features gave him the answer: *Most probably.*

Owen, Red, and Cort didn't know it, but they

weren't far behind Fargo and Marga: five and a half miles, to be exact.

"Stop!" begged Cort, who wasn't accustomed to traveling at this pace. These past few days, on horseback with Marga, had been the most uncomfortable in living memory. He wasn't used to riding, and he didn't care for it one bit.

Beside him, the brutish Red merely laughed. It was more like a donkey's bray, though, and Cort cursed him mentally. He couldn't afford to curse him out loud. Not right now.

"What's'a matter, Mr. Named-for-a-town-in-Iowa?" Owen shouted.

Ohio, you idiot, Cleveland thought.

They had been trotting these beastly creatures for an hour. Red's and Owen's horses might have had nice, comfortable gaits, but Cort's horse was an overpriced stable mount, short-coupled and sore-footed, and choppy at best.

"Food!" Cort proclaimed.

At the moment, he wasn't capable of more than single syllables, and he needed an excuse—any excuse—to get off this damned horse. Christ, he was going to be maimed for life!

"Sounds like a good idea, there, Cleveland," Red said, and Cort silently blessed his so-called insight. "I could use me some vittles my own dang self."

Owen, God bless him, reined his horse down into a walk, and Red and Cort followed suit.

"All right," Owen said. "Let's stop for a while." He patted his mount's neck. "Horses could use a break, too, I reckon."

Cort was out of the saddle and on the ground before he had brought his horse to a complete stop, and stood there, the muscles of his thighs and buttocks literally trembling.

When this is over, he thought, *if I never see another saddle again it will be too goddamn soon!*

Owen was a few feet away, loosening his horse's girth, but Red already had his saddlebags down. He rooted around inside them with a grubby hand, and finally pulled out a packet. After picking a few tiny rocks and taking something that looked like cobwebs off the contents, he held a stringy piece of dried meat toward Cort.

"Jerked badger?" Red asked as he stuck a second chunk in his mouth and happily began to chew.

Dear God, thought Cort.

But he made himself smile.

And he took it.

Owen stood aside, watering the horses and watching Mr. Cort Cleveland. Even though he had welcomed this greenhorn, urged him to join them on their quest to find Fargo, he wasn't sure about him.

At first, he'd figured Cleveland to be a gambler. The fancy clothes had led him to jump to that conclusion, as had Cleveland's definite lack of horsemanship.

But lately, he had changed his mind. Now he was thinking that maybe Cleveland was one of those shady confidence men who hung around train depots and such. Cleveland's being way the hell out here didn't make much sense, but he said he'd been traveling with a woman. Maybe she'd been the one to have a hair up her butt to see the West.

Well, all in all, it didn't much matter much, one way or the other. Owen Thurst still didn't exactly trust him.

Red? Now that was another matter. Ol' Red seemed to have taken to Cort Cleveland like a hog to slop. He'd even offered Cleveland some of that goddamn badger jerky. Filthy stuff.

Owen would rather eat jerked billy goat meat any day of the week. And in fact, he was eating it. Or would be, as soon as he finished with the horses.

"So this Fargo, he stole your woman, did he?" Owen heard Red ask, and he perked up a little.

"Yes," said Cleveland, who remained standing, although Red was stretched out on the ground, in the low, thin shade of a couple of creosote bushes.

His butt was sore, Owen thought, and stifled a nasty grin.

"How'd he do that?" Red asked.

"He showed up," replied Cleveland, in a tone that said he would brook no further questions.

But Red couldn't take no for an answer, implicit or otherwise. "Why'd he do that, then?" Red asked.

Cleveland rolled his eyes. "He just did," he said, a little peevishly. "All right?"

Well, if he dumped Red when this was over, and if Cleveland behaved himself, he might could use himself a smart new partner, Owen thought. 'Course, if he wasn't any use with a gun . . .

Mayhap he could teach Owen to be a confidence man. After all, a feller couldn't have too many skills out here.

Owen shrugged, and reached into his saddlebags for his own supply of jerky.

He'd see.

He had time.

In Quake, New Mexico, Diego Madrid and his wife, Rosa, sat in his study, as was their habit.

Rosa was quietly working on her fancywork, seated at the tilted frame, carefully stitching a pattern in blues and pinks. Madrid knew it stated "Home Sweet Home" in a fancy scrollwork at the top, and repeated the same phrase at the bottom, in Spanish.

Madrid, a cigar smoldering in the ash tray at his elbow, sat in a leather chair, reading what passed for a newspaper in this quiet hamlet.

He liked the fact that Quake was quiet. The town's

name was a lie, really, he thought. Nothing remotely Quake-like had ever happened in Quake, and he was content that it should stay that way.

Rosa, his beautiful Rosa, looked up from her needlework.

"Diego?" she said softly.

"Yes, my peach?"

"You haven't heard from Fargo again?"

"No, my dove," he said soothingly. "He is likely traveling where there is no telegraph. We will hear again, very soon."

She began to stitch again, then paused. "Diego?"

"Yes, my darling? What troubles you? You know Marga has done this many times. She will return. She always does."

"I know. I worry about your friend, Fargo."

Madrid stifled a chuckle. "Fargo does not need the help of your sympathy, my darling Rosa. He will do his job."

"I know, Diego," she said, and shuddered a bit. Madrid supposed that she was remembering her time with those filthy kidnappers. Again, he thanked his lucky stars that they had not touched her . . . in that way. But then again, Rosa would never allow it.

"Are you all right, my peach?" he asked softly.

"Yes," she said. "I do not worry so much for myself. Or even Fargo. I worry for—"

"I know," Madrid said, gently cutting her off.

There was silence between them for a moment, and then her pretty brow wrinkled and she asked, "Diego? You don't supposed that she has actually—"

"Perish the thought, dearest Rosa," he said, shaking his head solemnly. "Perish the thought."

12

"We'll stop here," Fargo said, and reined that fancy horse of his to a halt.

Marga was glad, because it was nearly all the way dark. Her horse had already stumbled twice and she was afraid that if it stumbled again, she would take a tumble. Her face was her fortune, after all. Well, at least a good part of it. She wanted to take no chances on bruising herself.

But on the other hand, she wasn't speaking to Fargo, and therefore couldn't voice her worries. Blast him, anyway! What was the matter with the man?

Half of the time, he acted as he should, as all men acted while they were under her spell. He was subservient, polite, willing, and could be easily guided to do her bidding.

But the other half?

It made her crazy! It was as if she had a bag over her head, as if she were, well, *ordinary!*

Marga did not care for being treated as if she were ordinary. Not one tiny bit. Even Cort Cleveland, with all his many faults, hadn't treated her this way!

She dismounted without waiting for Fargo's help. Frankly, she dismounted before he had a chance to help her, mainly because she was afraid that he wouldn't· offer and that she would thus be humiliated further.

He took the reins from her without a word, merely giving her a curt nod of acknowledgment, and led the horses away.

She sat down on a rock, then stood again. Oh, to have something soft to sit upon! She had not realized how much she would miss the comfort of a hotel room, even a poor one.

But then, she had thought that she would have the comfort of Fargo's arms to see her through the night.

She snorted softly, and lifted her chin.

That would be the day!

But then, she started thinking about that sweet, incredible bout of earlier lovemaking, and she felt herself beginning to soften. Fargo had been marvelous. She could think of no other word for it.

How she had wished that there had been more time, that they had both been naked instead of having their clothes bunched up between them like two young people in the back of a buggy. She wished that there had been time for small talk and lovers' murmurs, and that there had been time to repeat the whole proceedings.

An encore, as it were.

She sighed, and watched Fargo's back through the fading light as he fed and brushed the horses, yearning for him, aching for his touch . . .

No!

She steeled herself. She would not weaken. She would not give him another chance to humiliate her.

She was the divine Marga, after all, she thought. All men wanted her, damn it. All men groveled at her feet, worshiped at her shrine, begged for her slightest notice!

They most certainly did *not* have their way with her. At least, not to abruptly order her up on her goddamn horse again.

The nerve!

But despite her resolve, she was already staring at

him, already lusting for him, already imagining him atop her in the night.

A few miles back, Owen, Red, and Cort had stopped for the evening, and stopped early.

Mostly, this was on Cort Cleveland's account.

He lay beside the fire, alternately sipping at a flask of bourbon, rubbing his sore backside, and wishing that someone would kill Red.

"Har har," Red brayed at him, for the twentieth time since they'd stopped. "You're sure a jim-dandy, Mister Iowa."

"Ohio, damn it," Cleveland muttered. He was only correcting Red out of habit now. He didn't expect it to do any good whatsoever. After all, you couldn't give a fiddle to a frog and expect it to play "The Flight of the Bumblebee."

You could only hope that the damned frog didn't shit on it.

Furthermore, while he hadn't had high expectations of his traveling companions, to begin with, his hopes about them (meager as they were) had been dashed over the course of the day. At the moment, he was only daring to pray that Red had some sort of idiot savant ability with firearms.

It was quite obvious that cleverness would certainly have nothing to do with it.

"So," said Red, grinning like a fool—as if he knew any other way. "What you do for a livin', Cleveland? Bust broncs?"

Again, Red was overcome by his own keen wit, and collapsed into spasms of laughter.

Mercifully, Owen picked that moment to growl, "Aw, shut up, Red, and quit pickin' at him. Let Cleveland eat his beans in peace."

"Thank you," Cort muttered over Red's snicker, and scooped up another spoonful of watery, saltless, wallpaper paste beans.

He was wholly glad that it was dark. He didn't want too close a look at what he was eating. Chewing and swallowing was hard enough without having to stare at it, too.

He saw that Red was considering another comment, and he quickly asked, "Mr. Thurst—that is to say, Owen—you tell me you've been to the town of Chimney Ridge. What's it like? The populace, and so on."

"Not much," Owen replied, and slurped his coffee. "Wide spot in the road. 'Least, it was last time I was through."

"I ain't never been there afore," added Red. "Can't be much."

Cort ignored him. "It must have grown since then," he said to Owen, parroting what Marga had told him. "I'm assured that they have all the modern conveniences there. Even a theater."

Much to Cort's distaste, Owen burst out laughing, and spat beans across the fire in the process. "Theater? That's a laugh! The only stage they got in that town is when somebody stands on the back of a buckboard afore they hang him."

This sent Red into spasms of laughter. It did not, however, have any such effect on Cort Cleveland.

Frowning and gingerly brushing half-chewed beans off his waistcoat, he conceded, "I must have been misinformed, then."

But why would Marga have told him a lie about that? Why would she have any reason to? It didn't make sense.

Unless she had been lied to.

Well, that made no sense, either! How could any person in their right mind look into those bottomless, violet eyes, into that glorious face—the face of a goddess, an angel—and purposefully lie?

"Hell," continued Owen, "last time I was through there, they didn't even have the stage comin' through. Closest line was over to Flat Top, 'bout thirty miles

100

south." He held out his plate. "Ladle me up some more of them beans, Red. They's awful good tonight, even if there ain't no meat in 'em. How's your backside comin' along, Cleveland?"

"I'll be fine," Cort said. Dear God, he didn't care to think what kind of meat Red would have put in the beans if he'd had a chance. And had Owen said they didn't even have a stage line stopping through Chimney Ridge?

He couldn't imagine what on earth had possessed Marga to want to go there in the first place. If Logan were meeting her there—and Cort was already highly suspicious of this as yet unmet Logan, just on general principles—why would he have picked such a woebegone spot to do it in?

Why wouldn't he have chosen a town with, at the least, a stage depot?

My beautiful Marga is being played for a fool, he thought, at the same moment realizing—again—that she was no longer *his* Marga.

She was Fargo's Marga, now.

Damn him!

He determined that he would be better tomorrow. He would not make them call a halt to their travels early in the day. He would tough it through, ride into Chimney Ridge, and happily watch Red gun Fargo down.

And then, naturally, he would come to the stranded Marga's rescue and take her, well, wherever she wanted to go. And be with her again. That part was the sweetest to contemplate.

He had already forgotten the fights, the fits of rage, the name-calling, the looking down her nose, and his frustration with her. He only remembered her face, her figure, and the warmth of her flesh.

Once again, Marga would be his, and the hell with Fargo.

He raised his tin coffee mug. "To tomorrow, gentlemen," he said. "And to Mr. Red Neal's legendary skill with a gun."

Owen, grinning, raised his mug, too. "You got that right, Cleveland. To that son of a bitch Fargo, bitin' the dust."

"To me an' my Colt!" added Red gleefully, hoisting his cup with a great slosh of coffee.

They drank deeply, each for his own reasons.

"Why did you so mistreat me?"

The question startled Fargo, especially after such a long, long silence. They had ridden all afternoon, made camp, cooked and eaten their supper, all without a word except that which was absolutely necessary.

So he stared across the fire at Marga, one brow cocked, and said, "What? Mistreat you?"

"You heard me," she said. But she broke off the visual contact, and cast her eyes down.

Frankly, he'd been grateful that she'd been ignoring him. It sort of solved tonight's question—would she or wouldn't she?—and allowed him to yearn after her in safety, and from a distance.

An emotional distance, anyhow. But now this accusation, hanging in the air.

"That I did, Marga," he said guardedly. "But I didn't mistreat you. I'm keeping you safe, that's all." It was a bold-faced lie, and Fargo knew it. He supposed, belatedly, that Marga knew it, too.

But if she did, her expression didn't give her away. Her face didn't give away anything except that everlasting beauty.

She looked up at him once more, and this time, her countenance was angry.

No, he thought. *Peeved, that's it.* She was annoyed with him! Was that all he was to her? A bloody annoyance?

Slowly and with determination, she said, "After we finished . . . Afterward, you stood up—just left me there!—and got on your horse and ordered me to mount and follow you."

She sniffed derisively. "No one orders me around, Fargo. Not even you."

She tilted her nose in the air haughtily. Fargo sighed. She looked great, no matter what expression she had, no matter what attitude. No matter what or how she tried to make him feel, the only thing that actually got through to him was her startling beauty, and that fact that he wanted her.

No, needed her.

That must be one hell of a burden for a woman to bear, he thought, and then wondered where in the devil that idea had come from.

He usually wasn't much for introspection. He liked things plain and simple, reduced to their most basic, rudimentary terms. Right, wrong. Good, bad.

Of course, he rarely got them that way.

"Sorry," he said with a sigh, and lied again. "Didn't mean to make you feel that way."

He had, just a little. He'd been feeling used, and maybe he'd wanted her to suffer for it. But she hadn't done anything to him. She probably hadn't done anything that she hadn't done a thousand times before, although with different results.

Was this the first time anyone had made her feel just a little bit used, too? A little bit like a convenient back scratcher or bath sponge?

Suddenly, he was deeply sorry. Not so much for having done what he had done, but for making her upset, and perhaps making her question her own . . . He wasn't sure what. Worth? Appeal?

No, control.

"You've controlled every single situation you've ever been in, haven't you?" he asked, the words galloping out before he had a chance to think them over.

And he couldn't seem to shut the hell up. "You're the one who's always been in charge. Everybody

103

dances to your tune. Until today, that is. Isn't that the way things are, Marga?"

She tipped her head and stared at him, down her haughty little nose. "I beg your pardon, *Mister* Fargo?"

That did it. All the want and passion and bad temper that had been simmering through his veins since their noontime coupling suddenly came to a boil.

13

"That's it, isn't it?" he said, nearly roaring at her. "Jesus Christ, Marga! How can you be so beautiful and so . . . so . . . goddamn dense? All at the same time!"

She shot to her feet, knocking over the coffee cup that had been beside her. As her coffee hissed and turned to steam on the fire, she shouted, "How dare you! How dare you question me, accuse me? You are nothing to me! Nothing—do you hear?"

He was on his feet by this time, too, and stepped around the fire to grab her arm.

"You listen to me, you little witch," he said, his tone low, his voice intense, his eyes narrowed. "I've had about enough crud from you for one day. Where do you get off, going through the world like everybody in it is your servant? Who died and made you princess?"

Marga didn't say anything for a moment, but only stood there in his viselike grip, blinking rapidly. Obviously, nobody had ever pointed out these things to her before, although they were certainly true. Probably, no one had dared say a word.

Or had cared to.

Which gave Fargo something else to turn over in his head.

At last, he said, "Nobody ever cared enough to tell you, I reckon. Maybe they were afraid to—I don't know. And that's their fault, not yours. But baby doll, I'm going to tell you the truth, and right now. Honey, this high-and-mighty shit of yours can be a royal pain in the ass."

She blinked again, and this time her face was cloaked in fury. For once, it wasn't a pretty sight.

"How dare you!" she said, letting out the words in a snakelike hiss. "You are a nothing of a man. You are a gun for hire. You are beneath my feet!"

"Only when they're wrapped around me and locked behind my back, honey." He knew it was a low thing to say, but it was what he was thinking at the time, and he wasn't in the mood to couch his words.

She jerked her arm, and he let her slide free.

"Never!" she shouted, backing away. "Never have I been treated in such a fashion. Never have such words been spoken to me!"

"Then it's about time they were," he said calmly.

"My brother-in-law shall hear of this," she practically snarled. Her eyes flashed daggers in the firelight. "He shall have you flogged!"

Fargo snorted. This was getting funny, now. And he was beginning to feel like his old self. Finally!

Chuckling, he said, "Flogged? Diego Madrid's granddaddy might've had somebody flogged, but I'm afraid ol' Madrid is a little more modern than that. And what makes you think you'll ever see him again, anyway? Last I heard, Marga, you were running off to meet somebody named Logan, who I guess was going to take you away from all this."

He swept his arms out to the sides, indicating the desert: miles and miles of nothing but cactus and scorpions.

The calmer he became, the more upset and indignant she seemed to grow. Her brows knitted, her eyes narrowed, and she shouted, "Fine! I will not see Madrid or Rosa again!"

She suddenly bent down and picked up her coffee cup, then hurled it at him. He raised his arm, and it bounced off.

"Are you happy that you won on that point?" she screamed, and he thought that she was on the verge of hysteria. "Does it make you feel more like a man to browbeat a helpless woman?"

Fargo crossed his arms and shook his head, figuring that he'd best get her calmed down. "Marga, you are about the *least* helpless of any women I've ever met. Hell, every which way I turn, I see you getting exactly what you want. And that's power. You're not helpless. Not by a long shot."

Suddenly, some of what he'd said to her seemed to hit home, but he wasn't sure which part it had been. He braced himself for the worst.

But then, in a much lower voice, she said, "Yes. You are right, Fargo."

But that was all. He waited.

"I am sorry," she said finally, her voice sinking to a whisper. "I do have power. I have not been afraid to wield it, either. But you?" Her volume rose. "You are impossible!"

She cast her gaze to the ground, looking for something else to hurl at him.

He moved forward and grabbed her wrist, which forced her to turn her attention upward.

"*I'm* impossible?" he asked in disbelief. This girl really had a distorted view of things. "That's the pot calling the kettle black, isn't it? Is this what you and Cleveland fought about?"

"Of course not!" She tried to pull her arm away, but Fargo held her tight. "We argued about his gambling. We argued because he was a pig in bed. We argued over the stupid horses. But there was never— never!—any doubt about—"

"Who was in charge?" Fargo broke in.

Tight-lipped, she exhaled a little snort. Judging by

her expression, he half expected her to breathe out flames. She didn't answer him, though.

"That's what I thought," he said. "Well, Marga, I've got news for you. You won't be leading me around like an ox with a ring through its nose."

He paused, and decided that he'd get more with honey than with vinegar. He started over. "You're goddamn beautiful—I'll give you that much. I don't think I've ever seen such a beautiful woman."

She relaxed a little, and hoisted her brows in a way that said *tell me more*. But he didn't. He slowly began to swing the "conversation" more toward the point.

"But good looks can't cover up a spoiled, selfish little girl. Not for long."

She went stiff again.

"Marga," Fargo continued, "come morning, I'm turning us around. You've foxed me—I'll give you that—just like I reckon you've foxed every single man that's ever crossed your path. But it's not working anymore. Not on me, anyway. I'm taking you back to Quake and Diego Madrid and your sister's loving arms."

He added the bit about Rosa as an afterthought. He doubted very much whether Rosa ever showed enough emotion to be called loving.

Surprisingly, Marga began to cry. It wasn't a loud wail. It wasn't a fit of hysterics, which was what Fargo expected. Either that, or a slug to his chin.

Instead, it was as silent and slow as a spring thaw in Montana. A single tear welled over those thick, sooty lashes. It ran down her cheek and fell on her bodice, leaving a dark spot. It was followed by another, then another, and she never made a sound.

Her face softened, though. She looked absolutely shocked, as if he had just hauled off and punched her, or told her that her mama had died, or that her pet dog had been run over by a beer cart.

And for a moment, he actually believed it.

He gave his head a shake, as if to knock the sense back into it, and said, "Marga, that's not going to work, either."

"Pig!" she snapped, and the tears turned off as quickly as they had started. "Why won't you take me to Chimney Ridge? We're nearly there, Fargo!" Then, vitriolically, she spat, "Can't you stand me for one more day?"

He didn't say anything, just stood there, hanging on to her wrist. He was afraid that if he let go, she might try to grab his gun and shoot her way out. She was that desperate, if he was any judge. He reminded himself to sneak that little derringer of hers out of her handbag.

"Well, can't you?" she repeated, her voice growing shriller by the second.

"Tell me why you want to go," he said, a great deal more calmly than he felt at the moment. "It kind of pisses a man off not to know all the facts, you know. Especially when he thinks he's taking a woman to meet another man who maybe is going to bilk her. A man who's told her that there's a railroad and a goddamn theater in the middle of the Arizona wilderness."

Her brows shot up. "He—they—would not lie to me!"

"How do you know that?" Fargo continued. He had her attention now. For the first time since the fight had started, she was more interested in what he was saying than in her own reactions to it.

"Because . . . because he . . ."

"Because he's a man," Fargo said flatly. "And men don't lie to you."

She gave out a little huff. "Certainly not!"

"You know, Marga, I'm trying to be sarcastic, here, and you're taking me literally."

"What?" Her brows knotted again.

Fargo had found the second flaw in her armor—she

wasn't all that bright. Normally, he would have noticed a thing like that right off in a woman. Of course, normally, he wouldn't have all that beauty to be distracted by.

"Just who are 'they'? And what did this Logan character promise you, Marga?" he asked, as gently as he could.

"Nothing," she said warily. "Logan is only an agent."

"Of what?"

"Of the man who sent for me."

This thing was getting more convoluted by the second. Fargo took a deep breath and started again.

"All right," he said. "This man. The one that Logan works for. What's *he* want with you, then?"

Her nose tilted up in the air, and a smile spread across those beautiful lips. "He will make me celebrated in the capitals of Europe."

Fargo was totally at sea. All he could say was, "Huh?"

"Logan works for Mr. Carlos Sweeney," she said. When that didn't get a rise out of Fargo, she rather impatiently added, "The great impresario! He has heard of my singing! Logan will take me to San Francisco, where I will meet with Mr. Sweeney, who will make me a star of the opera!"

Now, Fargo had listened to her humming for a good half hour that morning, and it had been close to the longest half hour of his life. If she couldn't stay in tune any better than that, hell! She couldn't even nail down a job singing in a bar to drunken cowboys and miners, a group that wasn't exactly known for its musical discretion.

So the first thing that came out of his mouth was, "You have got to be joshing me."

"About which part?" she demanded, and then added stridently, "I assure you, I am deadly serious about every word of it."

"This Mr. Sweeney," Fargo said carefully. "He hasn't heard you himself?"

"Of course not!" she said. Her tone was a little too

patronizing for his taste, but he kept his peace. "I just told you, he had heard of my talent. Mr. Sweeney would certainly not travel . . . out here." A little shudder went through her when a coyote suddenly gave voice in the distance.

It sounded a whole lot better to Fargo than Marga's voice had, but again, he didn't say it out loud.

At last, he understood why Diego Madrid had that big, shiny piano, and why the walls were hung so thickly with heavy tapestries. They were there to muffle the sound when Marga practiced singing.

She must have a voice teacher, too, and at that moment, he had all of Fargo's pity. The poor son of a bitch probably had to stuff his ears with cotton.

The Madrid money could buy a lot of things, but it couldn't buy Marga a willing audience with unplugged ears. He doubted anything could, unless it was at a school for the deaf.

And he also doubted very much that this Sweeney fellow—if he even existed—was on the up and up.

And right then, at that very moment, he decided. "Marga," he said, "I'm going to take you to Chimney Ridge, after all."

He wouldn't be the one to tell her that she couldn't sing for beans, and that Sweeney was probably a ruse. He'd let this Logan make it abundantly clear. He half suspected that Logan had made up the whole thing about Sweeney, and that Logan was just trying to trick her, get her away from civilization. Arizona would sure be the place for that. It wasn't nearly so civilized as the old Spanish culture of New Mexico.

Just what Logan wanted to do with her once he got her out here, though, had Fargo a little worried. It made him mad, too.

And Fargo wasn't a man you made mad.

He let go of her wrist, at last.

She snatched it back and held it close to her breast, rubbing it.

"Why?" she asked suspiciously. Marga might think she was a woman of mystery, but her every expression showed on her face. Fargo supposed that most people were just too plain overcome with her to notice them. "Why have you changed your mind?"

Fargo shrugged. "I guess you persuaded me," he said, hoping she'd let it drop.

And she did.

"Oh," she said, and once again sat down beside the fire. She looked up at him through dark lashes. "Sit?" she asked, and patted the ground next to her.

No way in hell, Fargo thought, as he skirted the fire and sat down across from her, the flames in between. He said, " 'Fraid not, Marga. We're going to sleep separate tonight."

"Why?" Now she looked hurt. Jesus Christ! Was there no escape?

"Because I said so—that's why." Fargo felt like his mother for just a second. She'd repeated that damned phrase to him far too many times to count.

"You're being silly," Marga purred. The hand that had been rubbing her wrist moved to toy with the top button of her bodice. "We can still be friends. We can be more than friends, Fargo."

Fargo had told himself countless times that he wouldn't give in to her again, wouldn't be bewitched again, wouldn't be bamboozled by her looks and her obvious charms. He had warned himself until he was blue in the face—not to mention blue in the balls— and he wasn't, by God, going to cave in now.

"No," he said abruptly, and shook out his blanket. Using willpower he didn't know he had, he stretched out, turned his back on her, pulled his hat down low, and said, "Night, Marga."

He didn't believe his britches had ever felt so uncomfortably tight.

14

Fargo was mercifully halfway asleep when he was roused by a soft sound. Rustling.

He opened his eyes, not moving, preparing to do what needed to be done. The sound didn't get louder, though, didn't change.

It wasn't a coyote or a bear or a cat. Any one of those, invading camp, would have caused a whole lot more noise, including that of nervous or terrified horses trying to get away. But the Ovaro hadn't so much as whickered.

The sounds weren't soft yet clumsy, like sounds a man would make when he was trying to sneak up on somebody.

Marga?

He almost turned over, but then stopped. What if she were changing her clothes? Hell, he needed that like he needed a hole in his head. Just the idea of it was already swelling him and making his britches too tight again.

So he lay there a few more seconds, until the sound stopped. He let out a breath of air through pursed lips and tried to relax.

He almost did.

Until he felt a presence hovering near, and a small hand on his shoulder.

"Fargo?" Marga whispered gently. She was up, all right. And when he turned toward her, he saw that she was as naked, and as perfect, as one of those ancient Greek statues.

Holy Jesus.

Well, that did it. He could be a stoic man, but, by God, even he had his limits!

He pulled her down on top of him, and she came willingly, a smile tickling at her lips.

"I knew you could not resist," she whispered in his ear as the soft weight of her body came to rest atop his. "I knew you wanted me, my love."

She licked his face from jaw to temple with one sweeping caress of the tip of her tongue.

His pants were about to split, and he let go of her long enough to shove them down and out of the way. Goddammit—there was something magical about her, the way she could get him all riled up! He couldn't stand her, but right now, at this moment, he wanted her more than he'd ever wanted another woman.

She helped him kick his britches off, then helped in pulling off his shirt, and all the while he marveled at, lusted over, her body. It was perfect, flawless—not a single blemish, not a mole, not a birthmark, nothing but soft, creamy skin over full, rounded, upturned breasts and smooth thighs and lush hips.

The feel of it, under his broad hands, was like warm, inviting silk.

And then they were both naked, there in the firelight. Marga's hand skimmed over his chest, over his shoulders, and she licked her lips.

"You are as handsome—no, as beautiful—as I thought," she said, and her voice was full of hunger.

Her fingers trailed down his chest, past his waist, to take his member in her hand. Her fingers didn't quite go around him. "And Fargo, you are very big," she added with a purr. "Very large indeed."

"All for you, baby," he said, and rolled her over, onto

her back. He knew that if she touched him much longer he'd explode, and he wasn't quite ready to do that.

She spread her legs, and he pushed into her easily. She was wet and warm, as slippery as pond weeds in summer, and as welcoming as a hearth on a winter night. And more. She was alive—she was incendiary!—and it was clear that she wanted him as much as he wanted her.

She wrapped her arms around his neck, hugged his shoulders, combed her fingers through his hair, and she whispered, "Now, my Fargo, yes, now!"

He began to drive into her with powerful thrusts, more powerful than those he had expended that noon, and the strength of his movements lifted her off the ground. She laughed and groaned, all at the same time, as he rode her mindlessly but with purpose, feeling the fire in his own groin grow and grow and grow.

"Yes, yes!" she breathed, her eyes closed, her voice throaty with passion. "Yes, Fargo, yes!"

And he drove forward as her legs locked around his hips and he felt her smooth, slim thighs slithering over him. Higher and higher he rose, going upward toward release, traveling swiftly. The blood rushed through his ears so that he barely heard her when she said, "Now! Now!"

But something in him did hear her, because he gave a tremendous heave and a twist, and she climaxed with a scream that silenced the coyotes and the insects, and he felt himself tumbling, tumbling, tumbling . . .

He lay atop her, still embedded deep within her softness, panting, and she panted beneath.

"Christ," he finally muttered.

"Indeed," she gasped.

He felt her inner muscles teasing at him, squeezing and releasing him over and over, in the aftermath of her orgasm.

It felt good. It felt a whole lot better than a bad woman should make a good man feel.

But what the hell.

He rolled off her at last, and lay beside her, her head on his chest, her tiny hand resting on his flat belly.

"Wonderful," she said with a sigh. "You were absolutely wonderful. I knew you would be. Again. But this is so much nicer."

"Nicer?" he asked absently. He was beginning to feel that familiar tickle in his crotch. Her hand on his belly, hovering so near his already awakening groin, was definitely a contributing factor.

"You haven't ordered me on my horse, yet," she said, and when he looked at her, she was smiling.

He smiled back, somewhat sheepishly. "Sorry about that," he said. Right at the moment, he was. She could be human, after all. He gave her a little hug.

Her fingers crept downward and she took him in her hand.

"Fargo?"

"Yes?"

"I think you are growing again, my love."

He grinned wickedly. "By God, Marga, I think you're right," he said in pretended amazement, and kissed her.

Morning dawned, bright and clear, and found Fargo and Marge still entwined in each other's arms, and still quite naked.

Fargo yawned, carefully stretching his arms to avoid dislodging Marga, who had used his chest for a pillow. But she woke anyway.

"Good morning, Fargo, my love," she said in a whisper, and ran one sleek thigh up his leg, hugging him with it.

"Mornin'," he replied. Now, in the cold light of day, he was beginning to have second thoughts. Not that they'd do much good. What would happen next would happen, one way or another.

Marga rolled away from him, onto her back, and sighed happily. "Last night was the thing of fables, my dear," she said dreamily. "Four times, and each one different. You are superior to any other lover I have had, my pet. I swoon."

In spite of himself, Fargo chuckled. "No, you don't," he said. "You can't fool me. You were wide awake the whole time."

She laughed, and it was music. And then he remembered why she wanted to go to Chimney Ridge, and he frowned.

"What?" she asked, and propped herself up on one elbow. Her round breasts hung, full and ripe and beckoning him. "What is it?"

Hell, he couldn't tell her. As much as he wanted to, and as many times as he'd practiced in his head, he just couldn't.

He forced his frown into a smile. "Nothing, honey. Just thinkin' that we'd better be moving pretty soon—that's all."

"I suspected as much," she replied, then sighed. "Oh, well. In Chimney Ridge, there will be a grand hotel. And sheets. And pillows. And a down mattress." She grinned again. "That, I will look forward to."

She took his hand and placed it over one of her breasts. "And this," she said with a grin, "you will have this to look forward to. I noticed you paid them much attention last night. Especially the second time we made love. They like attention, you know. You make them happy."

He rolled toward her, bent his head, and took her nipple into his mouth. She sighed happily as he began to nuzzle and nurse her, then took the tip between his teeth and rolled it gently.

"Yes," she whispered, "like that, my love, like that."

He hadn't meant it to happen again this morning,

but before he knew it, he had come up into a sitting position and pulled her onto his lap. She sat, straddling him, and he eased her onto his staff.

She let out a long hiss, and delightedly whispered, "Again you surprise me, Fargo."

She arched her back, leaning into the strength of his supporting arm, and began to move her hips. Fargo ran his hand over her breasts, teasing them, toying with them, as she moved and swirled about him.

Her inner muscles were at play, too, and he felt her tug at him, push him, pull him as she moved. It was like being in the belly of a dancer, he thought.

He lowered his head and lapped at her breasts, first one, then the other; and then he ran his hand from her thick, lustrous hair down over her bosom to the juncture of her thighs.

And then the sensation of being inside her, as she swirled and wiggled and roiled sensuously, became too much for him.

He pulled her upright and held her tight while she moved faster and faster and faster, bringing him—and herself—to a speedy but extraordinarily satisfying climax.

"Marga," he breathed, still hugging her body—damp with perspiration—to his and feeling her final shudders move through him.

"Yes, love?" she replied, slick with sweat and panting.

"Get on your horse."

She jerked her head back, but she grinned at him widely and said, "Fargo! You are such a dog!"

They didn't stop long enough at noon to take advantage of the rest. Fargo saw to that. He knew damn well that once he got Marga naked, he lost all track of time. And he had a feeling that right now wasn't exactly the point to let that happen again.

Marga was disappointed, but when he explained it

to her, she saw the sense in it. This surprised him, because he had expected a fight. But she only said, "Very well, my love," and gave no further argument.

They rode into the outskirts of Chimney Ridge at around four thirty in the afternoon. It was actually a fair-sized little hamlet, thought Fargo in surprise, but it sure didn't have a theater. Or a railroad.

Marga was crushed.

"No!" she kept repeating as they rode up the main street. "But he promised!"

Fargo didn't say anything.

They left the horses at the livery and walked up to the hotel. By the looks of it, Fargo doubted there'd be any such thing as even a chicken feather mattress, let alone one stuffed with down, but he kept his mouth shut. He'd let the town speak for itself.

He wouldn't say *I told you so.*

Poor Marga already looked beaten down enough.

He actually felt sorry for her.

At the hotel, he signed the register for both of them. He noticed that she didn't inquire about Mr. Logan, and once they were upstairs, and he was putting the key into the lock, he asked, "I thought you were in a big hurry to see him."

"Logan?"

"Yes." He opened the door and ushered her inside. It was a nice room as far as hotels went, but just nice, not grand.

Hell, she must be past disappointed.

She went directly to the bed and slumped down on it, saying nothing. Fargo locked the door behind him, and then sat down beside her.

"It's all right, Marga," he soothed. "Maybe this Logan fellow didn't know about the town. Hell, he's likely here right now."

He couldn't believe he had just said it, but he had. And he had a terrible feeling that if Logan heard her

119

sing one lousy note—and he did mean lousy—he'd flee on the next stage. If Chimney Ridge had one, that is.

"They have lied to me," Marga said, on the edge of tears. "I cannot believe that anyone would tell me an untruth!"

And there it was again. She couldn't fathom that anybody could take one look at her and fib. It just wasn't in her experience.

Fargo put his arm around her. "We'll see, honey. I'll go down and check at the desk."

She sniffed, but she didn't look up at him. "Thank you, Fargo. I couldn't bear to do it myself."

15

At right around six, Owen Thurst, Red Neal, and Cort Cleveland rode into Chimney Ridge, too. Cort led his horse in. It had pulled up lame about three miles out of town, and frankly, he had been relieved when Owen "suggested" to him that he dismount and lead it the rest of the way.

Except that now his legs were as sore as his poor backside. He couldn't win.

But when they got to the livery, he was suddenly feeling better, in spirit if not in flesh. There stood the gelding he'd bought for Marga, and that flashy paint stallion of Fargo's.

Owen stood glaring at the Ovaro, clutching at the top board of the stall's wall. "I oughta just kill this damned nag," he grumbled. "Serve Fargo right."

Owen raised a hand as if to reach out and strike the horse, and surprisingly, the paint snaked out his head and tried to bite it.

Owen jumped back. "Goddamn Injun pony! They bites, all of 'em!"

Cort put his hand on Owen's shoulder before any more damage was done. "Come along, now. We know he's in town. That they're both in town," he added softly, more to himself than Owen.

"Yeah!" piped up Red. "What you wanna do,

Owen? You want I should just gun him right off, or you want to play with him a mite?"

Owen scratched the back of his head, tipping his hat forward in the process. "Ain't sure, Red," he said. "Ain't got that far in my thinkin'."

Cort spoke up. "If I may suggest," he said, "we could retire to the saloon. I don't know about you gentlemen, but I, for one, am parched."

It was the truth, too. Also, he was well aware that they played cards at any saloon. That had a certain amount of pull, as well.

Owen appeared to be relieved. "Sounds good, Cleveland. Let's go up and have a drink and think it over. Fargo's one tricky bastard. I'd hate to let him get away on me again."

"But why can't I just gun him?" Red said as they walked out of the livery and started up the street. "That wouldn't take no time at all, and then we could go to the saloon."

Owen smacked the brim of Red's hat, which caused Cort Cleveland to jump a few inches.

"Because," Owen said, "once we gun him, we'll have the sheriff and everybody else in town after us—that's why. I ain't gonna dodge a hail'a bullets just so's you can have a beer, you damned fool."

Cort felt a sudden pang of fear shoot through him, And it wasn't just because Owen had brought home the reality of all those angry townsfolk, who would be riding after them for probably miles and miles and miles once the deed was done.

No, it was the idea that Owen was going to yell at Red one time too often, and that Red would then refuse to kill Fargo.

"There, there, Owen," he said hurriedly. "I'm sure that Red is aware of that."

Owen sniffed. "Hell, you got to remind him every fifteen seconds."

"No, you don't," said Red indignantly.

Rather than making things worse, Cleveland put a large smile on his face and threw an arm around each of the smelly creatures. His eyes threatening to water from the fumes, he said jovially, "Let's go and have ourselves a drink, boys!"

"Sure!" said Red, as if the subject had never come up before.

Owen just growled, but he came along.

Another crisis averted, Cleveland thought, as he kept that phony smile plastered to his face. *Dear Lord, how soon will this be over?*

And in his mind, he kept on picturing the ultimate prize.

Marga.

Fargo rapped at the door of Room Twelve, where the desk clerk had told him he could find Mr. Clive Logan.

The silver-templed, dark-haired man who answered his second knock was about six feet tall and well dressed and well groomed, but a tad rumpled, as if Fargo had just disturbed his afternoon nap.

The man yawned, confirming Fargo's suspicions, and sleepily said, "Yes?"

"Logan?" Fargo asked.

The man hoisted one brow and smoothed his oiled hair back into place. "And who wishes to know?"

"I'm Skye Fargo, Mr. Logan," Fargo began again. "I'm here to talk to you about Marga Trentwell-Oberon."

Logan nodded, but didn't offer to open the door any wider. "So where is the little tart?" he asked, appearing bored. "I was told she'd be in town by the time I arrived. I have been here in this dismal hamlet for three unbearable days, and she still has yet to make an appearance."

Fargo's brows knitted. The little tart? He asked, "Just what kind of a deal is this, anyway, Logan?"

"I would suggest that before I explain that to you," Logan said, "you tell me what you have to do with her." And then he studied Fargo's face more closely, and skimmed a quick look over his buckskins. His features bunched. "Did you say your name was . . . ?"

"Fargo."

Logan's eyes opened a little wider. "No. I mean to say, not *the* Fargo! The Fargo they call the Trailsman? The one they write stories about?"

"I reckon," Fargo admitted somewhat sheepishly. This was a man from the city, not a real westerner, and so the only place he would have become familiar with that Trailsman moniker was in the nickel books.

And Fargo wasn't fond of the nickel books, not one whit.

So it wasn't much of a surprise when Mr. Clive Logan broke out laughing. "Dear God!" he said between whoops. "The pulp writer's dream stands in my doorway, in the flesh! Deerhide clothes and all!"

Fargo put his hand on the door and pushed. Logan was shoved back a foot, and he stopped laughing right away. Backing up, he put his hands up in front of him, palms out, and quickly said, "I meant no offense, old boy. Please!"

Sweat had instantly broken out in beads over his forehead, and Fargo took pity on him.

"None taken," Fargo said, although he halfway growled it. He said, "About Marga?"

Logan produced a handkerchief from his pocket and dabbed at his forehead. "Yes, certainly. Miss Trentwell-Oberon."

"You're here to meet her, right?"

"That is correct."

"Something about making her an opera star?"

Logan snorted derisively. "Oh, I very much doubt that."

Fargo sighed. He pointed to a chair. "Sit down, Mr. Logan. I think I see a long conversation coming on."

Logan seated himself, then looked up warily. "You're not going to kill me or . . . something?"

" 'Course not," Fargo replied with a frown. What did this fancified fool think he'd do, anyway? Tar and feather him? Hang him from the nearest cottonwood? "You've been reading too many of those half-dime books, Mr. Logan. I just want some answers."

Logan breathed an audible sigh of relief and took a last swipe at his forehead. Tucking the handkerchief back into his pocket, he said, "Then, sir, you may address me as Clive."

Cort Cleveland was deep into a possible full house when Owen came up behind him.

"C'mon," Owen said gruffly. "Let's go."

Cleveland held up one finger. "A single moment longer, sir," he said. Frankly, he was getting sick and tired of being so damned polite—especially with these pigs—but he'd started it that way, and now he had to play it out.

Owen stood there behind him for perhaps half a minute before he said, "That's a mighty good hand you got there, Cleveland. Two pair!"

Immediately, everyone at the table grunted or swore, and threw their cards in. Cleveland closed his eyes and counted to ten. When he opened them at last, he scooped up his meager winnings—the pot could have been so much bigger!—and turned to face Owen, who was chuckling.

"Get your attention, there, Cleveland?" he said, still laughing.

Cort Cleveland did the absolute last thing he expected to do. He drew back and slugged Owen Thurst square in the jaw.

Owen wasn't out, but he hit the floor with a loud thud and glared up at Cleveland. "What'd you do that for, you lopsided son of a bitch?" Owen demanded, rubbing his jaw.

"Never meddle with a gentleman's game of chance," Cleveland said, in what he considered his best, most-cultured voice. He hoped to hell that Owen—or Red—wouldn't take a dislike to him. He'd hate to be gunned down just for a lapse in taste.

All right, for his stupidity.

But Red, God bless him, just rocked back and forth on his heels and smiled like it was Christmas morning.

"Never," Cleveland repeated sternly. And then he put down a hand to help Owen up.

Owen took it and climbed to his feet. But there was something in Owen's eyes that told Cleveland that he *had* gone too far. Owen had just decided to wait to get even—that was all. And he'd probably tipped the odds in his favor, too.

He'll probably shoot me while I'm asleep, Cleveland thought dismally. *Why the hell did he have to come up and bother me when I had the first good hand I've held in days?*

He looked down at his pot. Couldn't be more than four dollars at the most. These idiots! He and Marga had best leave town as fast as possible, and they'd best leave these lunatics in their dust.

And then he remembered.

Marga.

He pocketed the coins. Turning toward the table, he tugged the brim of his hat. "Gentlemen," he said to the players. "A good evening to you all."

"Yeah," said a cowpoke in a grimy blue shirt, who had been seated across from him. "Come back anytime and bring your money, dude. And your friend, there."

The other players thought this was very funny. Cleveland ground his teeth, but walked out of the saloon. Once on the sidewalk, he turned to Owen again and growled, "What?"

Owen snorted. "Just tryin' to tell you, Cleveland. We got a plan."

"How nice for you," Cleveland snapped. And even as he said it, he knew he was digging his grave deeper. He just couldn't seem to help himself.

More than anything, he wanted to go back into that saloon and sit down at that poker table again. Well, *almost* more than anything. There was Marga . . .

He sighed. "What is it?"

Red moved to the fore. Excited, almost gleeful, he began, "See, me and Owen been talkin' about it, and we figure—"

Owen shoved him out of the way. "I'll tell it," he said. "We figured you was right in the first place. You may talk like a dandy, but I reckon you got your smarts about you."

"Thank you," said Cleveland, and he thought that this must be the speech you gave a man just before you killed him. "Go on."

"Well," Owen said, "we figure to just go on up to the hotel and blast him. Me and Red, that is. You're supposed to go down to the livery and get our horses."

Cleveland frowned. "Mine's lame." Were they planning to leave him behind? But then, he reminded himself, he *wanted* to be left behind! He'd be in town; Marga would be in town; Red and Owen would be long gone and Fargo would be dead.

What could be better?

"I see where you're going with this," Cleveland said quickly, before Owen or Red had a chance to speak up. "You wish me to remain behind. Yes, yes, very clever of you."

This last remark seemed to give Owen pause.

Not Red, though. "We are?" he piped up.

"Certainly, certainly!" Cleveland said, nodding enthusiastically. "Most devilishly clever!"

"Owen?" said poor Red, obviously at sea.

But Cleveland's initial take on Owen—that he was dumb, but would never admit to it—proved correct. Thank the Lord.

Owen said, "Shut up, Red. You're damned right it's clever, Cleveland. I know what I'm doin', all right. Now, go fetch our broomtails and lead 'em out back of the hotel."

"Certainly, Owen," Cleveland said, keeping his face stoic and serious. "Right away."

And he held his expression in that manner halfway to the livery, when he burst into laughter.

16

Fargo closed Clive Logan's door softly behind him before he leaned against the wall and put his hand to his forehead. It was as he expected, only worse, if that were possible.

Logan, who turned out to be an honest man and a reasonable sort, had explained it to him with an embarrassed shrug, saying, "I am sorry to admit it, Fargo, but it's my job. A distasteful part of my job, but a part of it nonetheless."

It seemed that the "famous impresario," Carlos Sweeney, was the real ticket, after all. He ran his opera company out of London, but it performed over three continents. He picked up new talent as he traveled with the company.

However, Mr. Sweeney—a half-Irish, half-Spanish rogue, as Logan called him—had a distinct weakness for the fairer sex. It was not beneath Mr. Sweeney, Logan told Fargo, to claim admiration for a young girl's voice when it was really what was under her dress that he was after.

"But the opera never comes to New Mexico," Fargo had said.

"It matters not," Logan had replied. "He heard of her. He heard she had a penchant for singing, and that she was a great beauty. A timeless beauty, in fact.

It was enough for him. He was looking for fresh game, as it were."

"Well, I'm sorry to tell you, but this 'fresh game' couldn't carry a tune if you nailed it to a board," Fargo had said, shaking his head.

"I believe he was counting on that," Logan had replied, nodding sadly.

So now Fargo stood in the hall, trying to figure out what to tell Marga. Now, he could tell her the truth. That would be the easy way out. She'd probably pitch one of her fits, then march down the hall and try to murder Clive Logan.

Or at least scratch his eyes out.

Neither probability exactly sparkled in the sunlight of Fargo's mind.

He could tell her that Logan was killed on the way to Chimney Ridge. But then, wouldn't she just want him to take her the rest of the way to San Francisco, where she could meet the Big Man in person?

Bad idea.

Well, he wasn't getting anywhere by just standing here, thinking. He'd take her to dinner. Maybe something better would occur to him.

He walked down the hall and rapped at his door. Marga answered with a soft "Come in, Fargo."

"How'd you know it was me?" he asked, smiling.

"Wild guess," she said with a little smirk. "Did you find Mr. Logan?"

"I did," he replied, nodding. "Want to go to dinner?"

"I'd rather have a bath," she said. "And more than that, I'd like to know where Mr. Logan is. And what he said. About me."

Her voice rose a little, and Fargo knew he'd best cut her off—or at least distract her—pretty quickly. He decided on distraction.

"First things first," he said, trying to smile wide and

for the most part succeeding. "Why don't you," he said, drawing her up, "go get yourself a bath. I think they've got one downstairs for fifty cents. And I'll go over to the barber shop and have one myself. I'll meet you back here, and then we'll go to dinner and I'll tell you all about Mr. Logan."

He was charming enough to waylay her, it turned out. She smiled at him and said, "All right, my handsome man. I should like to be clean before I deal with Mr. Logan. What's he like, anyway?"

Fargo pursed his lips, thought a moment, then said, "Stuffy, I guess."

"I thought as much," said Marga with a giggle, and picked up her satchel. She leaned toward him. "I have a fresh frock in here. I shall wear it for you tonight, my love."

She paused. "And then I shall take it off for you." she said slyly.

With a sigh, Fargo settled down into the barber shop's hot bath and felt his tired bones relax. He had a whiskey at his elbow, a cigar in his mouth, and the steaming fog to help him think.

And he surely needed to think: What to do with Marga?

He puffed leisurely at the cigar. He figured this was the last chance he'd have to do anything leisurely for a few days, anyway.

And they'd be long days.

Cort Cleveland led Red's and Owen's horses up the street, then around the back of the hotel. He tethered them in the alleyway, and then, whistling, walked down toward the barber shop.

What better alibi than to be naked in a bathtub when the deed was done?

* * *

The smitten desk clerk had hauled water and filled the hotel's tub for Miss Marga. She'd insisted that he call her that. Imagine!

Why, he'd never seen anybody so beautiful in all his born days, not even in a catalog or a magazine, not even in a painting. Dreamily, he leaned against the front desk, his chin propped in his hand. She was in there right now, naked!

Well, he thought, it would be kind of silly for a body to take a bath with their clothes on. He shook his head. But it was her. And she was in there, stark naked. In his hotel!

And then, out of nowhere, she began to sing.

At least, that's what he thought it was. He'd never heard such an ungodly racket in his life! Trying to hold his ears and grab a few spare towels at the same time, he walked quickly down the back hall, toward the bathing room. He jammed the towels against the base of the door, but they didn't do much good.

He thought about calling out and asking her to stop, but then, how could he tell a pretty woman—the prettiest woman he'd ever seen!—to shut the hell up before she broke his ears!

He ran back up the hall, closing connecting doors as he went, and finally gained the lobby again. He slammed the final door, which muted her off-key warble enough so that he guessed he wouldn't go crazy, and then he turned around.

He had customers.

"Can I help you gents?" he asked, and prayed that either they couldn't hear very well or they were tone deaf. He could still hear her faintly, even through all four of the closed doors between them. She could surely project, dammit.

"Yeah," said the dark, thin one. He turned the register around and began to peruse it. "You got a feller stayin' here, name of Fargo?" he asked. He didn't look up from the names. He also didn't seem to mind that awful screeching in the background.

"We do," the clerk said.

The redheaded one's face was screwed up and twisted, though, as if he were in pain. The clerk understood that, all right.

The redheaded man asked, "Who the hell's tryin' to sing back there? Hell, I can't understand a word of it."

"A patron. And I believe it's Italian, sir. I'm sorry."

A rough hand grabbed him by the collar and jerked him halfway across the counter. The dark man with the rough hand growled, "Well? Where are they? Where's he at, anyhow? Which room?"

The clerk thought fast. He didn't think it would do too well for him to point out Fargo's presence at the barbershop. After all, you didn't rent somebody a room and then see mischief done to them. On purpose, anyhow. And the lady? Even if she sounded like a screech owl, he sure wouldn't want to see a beautiful thing like her harmed in any way.

So he pointed up the stairs toward their empty room and said, "N-n-number nine."

Suddenly, the hand released him. He slid back to the other side of the desk, gulping and coughing, while the dark man and his redheaded friend drew their guns and started stealthily up the stairs.

Red tripped over Owen's spur just before they came to the top of the stairs, and he fell down with a thump and a thud.

"Quiet!" hissed Owen, who couldn't understand what he had ever done to be saddled with two such partners. Red was bad enough, but now this Cleveland? He'd thought about maybe taking Cleveland on, showing him a few ropes. But lately, all that fancy talk was really wearing thin. He didn't believe he could take that, coming across the campfire every morning.

But Red was so goddamn dumb!

"C'mon, dammit," he whispered loudly. Grabbing Red's arm, he yanked him up to his feet. "And be careful! Jesus, Red, they're gonna hear us sneakin' up here!"

Red shook his head like a dog coming out of the river. Probably shaking some sense back into it, Owen thought. And then he thought that Red could never shake it enough.

"I 'bout busted my ass, Owen," Red complained crankily. Looking pained, he rubbed his thigh with the muzzle of his gun.

"You're gonna shoot your damn knee off," Owen grumbled. "C'mon."

They crept down the hallway until they came to number nine. Silently, they took up positions on either side of the door, their guns raised. Adrenaline coursed through Owen's veins.

That son of a bitch Fargo was about to be his.

Red nodded his readiness, and Owen jumped in front of the door, kicking it open.

Both men entered, firing rapidly.

But Owen let Red go first.

Owen wasn't *that* stupid.

Fargo finished his bath, although it wasn't as leisurely as he would have liked ordinarily. For one thing, he kept thinking about what he was going to tell Marga—the exact way he'd phrase it.

For another thing, he kept thinking about, well, Marga in general.

He climbed out of the tub and toweled himself off, then donned his spare bucks. They were a little cleaner than the ones he'd been wearing for the past few days, anyway. While he was at the mirror, trying to see through the steam to trim his beard, he heard the distant pops of guns firing. It sounded like all hell was breaking loose somewhere or other.

Now, normally, he would have rocketed out of that barbershop and headed up the street to see what was going on. But this wasn't exactly a normal day. He merely stopped for a moment, listening, and then went back to his beard.

He was finished shortly, though, and stepped out front to pay the barber. While he waited for his change, he noticed that the door to the other bathing room was closed, and that steam was issuing from beneath the door.

"Busy night?" he said to the barber.

"Yup," came the reply, along with his fifteen cents. "Fellers like to get cleaned up when they come in off the trail."

Fargo nodded, pocketed the coins, and went on his way. But when he neared the hotel, he saw that a small crowd had gathered outside.

His brow furrowed, he pushed his way through the throng and into the lobby, just in time to see Owen Thurst and some redheaded yahoo come down the stairs. They were both in handcuffs, and they both looked madder than a bagful of bobcats.

When Owen saw Fargo, he shouted, "You! God-damn you, Fargo!"

"You was supposed to be upstairs!" hollered his red-haired companion. And then he turned toward Owen and whispered, just loud enough for Fargo to overhear, "That's him, right, Owen?"

Owen let out a wordless growl as the sheriff pushed them into the lobby. He paused and, around a wad of tobacco, said, "You're Fargo?"

"Last time I checked," Fargo said. "What'd you get Owen for?"

"Shootin' up a hotel room." The sheriff paused to take aim at the spittoon. "You oughta be right glad you wasn't in it. Tore the place up, these two. You say one of 'em's named Owen?"

"Owen Thurst," said Fargo, who was still taking in

the fact that they'd shot up his room. Thank God that nobody had been in it. Especially Marga.

The sheriff scratched his ear thoughtfully. "Sounds familiar. I might maybe have paper on him. Well, come on up to my office when you get time and give me a list of anything they wrecked. Tomorrow'll be all right. These boys've made me late for my supper as it is."

And with that, he moved out on the street, called back to the clerk, "Thanks for the heads-up, Archie!" and gave old Owen a little prod with the nose of his gun.

The desk clerk was already shooing the spectators out of his lobby. "Sorry, sir," he said to Fargo as he closed the door on the last of the onlookers. "I'll move you to a fresh room."

"Be obliged, Archie," Fargo said. "Where's the lady?"

"Still in the water, I reckon."

That was a relief, although Fargo thought it was a little odd that she hadn't come out to check on all the noise.

The clerk handed him a new key. "Room Seven," he said. "I'll send the lady up when she's ready."

Fargo tossed the key in the air, then caught it with one quick motion of his arm. "You do that, Archie."

17

At the café, Fargo seated Marga, then sat down opposite her. She was in a pretty dress, all frilly with extra bows and doodads, and the color of icy violets.

She was perhaps a little less fresh than when she had left her bath, but that was Fargo's fault. When she'd come back upstairs, all moist and dewy, her damp hair piled up in a towel, it had been too much for him. He'd taken her right then and there.

Or maybe she'd taken him. It was getting to be a real toss-up.

So in many ways, it was a satisfied Fargo who sat down across the table from the beauteous Marga. Owen and his sidekick were safely in jail and the room they'd shot up to put themselves there had been vacant. Marga was fit as a fiddle, and less upset than he'd thought she'd be about somebody using their room for target practice. And good Lord, she'd been fine in bed!

Down or not, that mattress was a lot nicer than the rocks they'd pulled up the night before—that was for sure. He was looking forward to the after-dinner festivities, too.

The waiter came over and they ordered, and then Marga asked the one question Fargo had been dreading. Actually, he'd been dreading it so much that he'd nearly put it out of his mind.

Until right now.

"Are you going to tell me?" she asked brightly. "Or are you going to make me beg?" She cast him a sly smile over the rim of her water glass. "You are good at that, you know, my darling."

"Well, Marga, it's like this," he began, then found he could go no further.

Her brow creased prettily. "It's like what, exactly?" she urged.

He started ahead, fully realizing that this might mean he'd sleep in separate quarters tonight. "Marga, I went to talk to your Mr. Logan."

"Yes," she said impatiently. "I know that, Fargo. What did he say? What of Mr. Sweeney? When is he taking me to California, to San Francisco? When would he like to hear me sing?"

Fargo gulped at that last question. But he decided that the truth needed to be told. He didn't exactly want to be the one to do it, but it seemed like he had no choice in the matter.

"Marga," he began, "I've got bad news for you."

Just then the waiter appeared with their supper, and Fargo held off saying anymore until the man had slid big plates of roast beef and fried potatoes and green peas in front of them.

"Bad news?" asked Marga, and her eyes nearly simmered. She hadn't so much as glanced at her steaming dinner.

Fargo sighed. "Sweeney's a big shot—you were right about that. But he's never heard you sing."

She sniffed. "I knew that already. He will hear me in San Francisco."

"No, he won't," Fargo said. "He's a . . . he's what they used to call a rake, Marga. He never heard a word about your singing, other than that you took some lessons. He wants you for a bed partner—that's all. An-

138

other trophy. Logan—who turned out to be an all-right fellow—has been on these little forays before."

"But once he hears me sing . . ." Marga began.

"Honey, that won't help," Fargo said. "Trust me."

Anger—white-hot—flickered over Marga's face, then settled there. "I beg your pardon, Mister Fargo? What do you know of my singing, anyway? Have you ever heard me? I'll have you know that Mr. Ethan Posthelwaite, the greatest voice teacher west of the Mississippi, has been tutoring me privately for the past five years! According to him, I am the finest mezzo-soprano the territory of New Mexico has ever produced!"

Fargo book a bite of his beef. He figured this might be the only chance he would get. He swallowed, then sat back in his chair. "Now, I don't mean to be flip, honey. But honestly, how many mezzo-sopranos—whatever that is—do you figure New Mexico has produced in total?"

She said nothing, just glared at him.

"I figure it's got to be slim to none," he went on. He thought about taking her hand but she'd probably just jerk it away, so he resisted. "Marga," he said, "I saw your practice room there at Diego Madrid's suite in Quake."

She gave her head a funny little tilt, as if to say, "And?"

"You ever notice how they got those walls padded with rugs and tapestries?" he asked. "I figure it's to cut the sound down."

"Well, of course it is!" she snapped indignantly. "It would drive anyone but a connoisseur of the opera mad with lack of understanding. And my sister and her husband are hardly aficionados of the arts," she added with a sniff.

"Why, they talk about me behind my back!" she went on. "My dear Rosa says I couldn't carry a tune in a bucket, which will show you how much she knows." She rolled her eyes.

Fargo suddenly had a new appreciation for ol' Rosa. "Baby," he said gently, "she's right. You been fooling yourself. I never heard you sing, but—"

"Of course you haven't, you swine!"

"But I heard you humming on the trail this morning, and it would have made a barn cat in heat crazy with the noise."

There. He'd said it. He hoped God—and Marga—would take mercy upon his soul.

But Marga stood up all of a sudden, and slapped her napkin down on the table. "Liar!" she practically barked. Her entire body shook with fury.

And then she simply turned on her heel and walked out of the restaurant.

Fargo sat, looking after her. She was headed up toward the hotel, at any rate. That was a good sign that at least she wasn't going to do something stupid, like take off on her own.

He considered going after her. He even stood up. But in the end, facing her wrath was the last thing he wanted to do on a growling stomach.

Still standing, he realized that the restaurant was quiet—no sounds of clinking flatware or rattling china—and he looked at the seated crowd around him. To a man and a woman, they all sat stock-still, staring at him, not eating. Some had forks poised in midair.

Well, he supposed Marga had been a touch on the loud side.

He smiled and said, "Go on ahead with your supper, folks. Show's over." And then he sat down.

"For now," he muttered as he picked up his fork.

Well, anyway, dinner wasn't a total loss. The beef was awfully good.

I will kill him, Marga thought, as she stormed up the walk. *I will see him dragged through the cactus thorns! Boiled in oil! Drawn and quartered!*

She slammed into the lobby, giving the desk clerk

a jolt, and suddenly stopped. "Today, when I was singing. You heard me, didn't you?"

The clerk's face took on a pained expression, and he said, "Y-yes, ma'am."

"Well?" she demanded. "Did it sound off-key to you?"

The expression became almost tortured. "Um, actually, ma'am, it did sound sort of . . . strange."

She made a strangled sound in the back of her throat and shouted, "Why should I expect a bunch of . . . a bunch of *stupid* backwater desert rats to know anything about grand opera!"

She stormed up the stairs.

But when she came to their new room, she paused. She would certainly not spend another night in Fargo's presence! She turned to go back down the stairs, then thought better of it. She turned around, and a smile touched her lips.

She would hear, from the horse's mouth, as it were, just what exactly was going on. Fargo must be lying. He must have some reason to lie that she wasn't aware of. Perhaps Madrid had paid him to not only bring her back, but to dash her dreams once and for all.

She could not imagine that he would be so cruel after last night. But he was, and he had been, all along.

She walked up the hall, to Room Twelve and Mr. Logan, and raised her arm to knock. But she paused with her knuckles inches from the wood. What if Fargo hadn't been lying? What if he had told her the truth?

A chill ran through her.

No. Nonsense! He had lied, and that was all there was to it.

She rapped at the door.

Cort Cleveland nearly walked right into the restaurant and Fargo's lap.

But he had the sense—or perhaps the luck—to

glance in through the window before he entered, and what he saw gave him pause. Not to mention a near heart attack.

There sat the "late" Fargo at a table for two, eating a solitary dinner.

Cleveland couldn't imagine what had happened! He had expected to bide his time, to wait a decent interval, and then turn up at the hotel. He would have been so surprised to find Marga there, alone and needing him. He would have been such a great comfort to her.

But there sat Fargo!

Outside, on the walk, Cleveland put a hand out to lean on the side of the building, then managed to get himself over to a wide sill, two doors down, before he slumped into a sit.

Damn the man! Did he have more lives than a cat?

It didn't cross Cleveland's mind to wonder about Owen Thurst and Red Neal, except to curse them for not doing what they had promised.

Idiots!

Now what was he supposed to do? Shoot Fargo himself? He was as ill-prepared for that contingency as he was to flap his arms and fly away to St. Louis.

He was no good with a gun—unless it was by stealth and his quarry was by far Fargo's inferior—and he knew it.

He sighed. First things first. He was a man with common sense if he was nothing else, he told himself, although hooking up with Owen and Red and not fleeing directly to the comforts of the East rather belied that statement. But it was what he told himself, and he felt better for it.

He would wait for Fargo to finish his goddamn dinner. That was the first thing. And then he'd go in and have some dinner himself.

And think about what to do next.

Yes. That sounded good.

*　　*　　*

"I'm very sorry, Miss Trentwell-Oberon," Clive Logan said most sincerely. "Those . . . those are the facts of it." He'd been licking his lips and stammering slightly even since he'd answered her knock. But then, she was accustomed to this reaction.

She hadn't been quite ready for what he told her about Mr. Sweeney, though, even though she'd already heard it from Fargo. She'd listened to the rest of it in a daze.

"But I would be happy to hear you sing," he added, and this most certainly got her attention. "I personally audition all of Mr. Sweeney's potential talent. And I do not mean for the, uh, bedroom."

"You would?" she said. "How very kind of you." She gave him a smile, and she would have sworn that he nearly melted into his chair. "Please call me Marga," she added, and he blushed bright red.

He stood up with some difficulty—she was accustomed to this from men, too—and made his way over to the bureau in his room. From the top drawer, he produced a shiny silver tuning fork.

Marga stood up and straightened her back, assuming her best singing posture.

"I realize that you have had no opportunity to warm up your voice," Mr. Logan said apologetically. He was still in a bit of a state. "But perhaps we could just run through a few scales and so on?"

"Certainly," she said, nodding.

"Very well," Logan said, holding the tuning fork aloft. She noticed that his fingers trembled. "I am prepared to be amazed," he said.

And with that, he tapped the tuning fork.

Marga began to sing as if her entire future depended on it.

It did.

Over at the jail, Owen and Red had refused to answer any of the sheriff's questions, including those regarding what day it was and who was running the White House at the moment.

The sheriff had finally left in disgust, announcing that they weren't worth his wife's burning the roast to a goddamn cinder; and now they sat there, watching the night deputy threaten to doze off in his chair.

Red, sitting across the single cell from Owen, said, "Why come we bein' so nice to let him sleep like that? Seems to me we could—"

"Sh!" hissed Owen, and slapped his cellmate with his hat. "Keep your damn voice down!"

The deputy, a young fellow far too full of himself to live, if you asked Owen, stirred in his chair and opened one clear, blue eye.

"You boys gettin' restless over there?" the deputy asked. "Now, if you're fixin' to talk, I'll go fetch Sheriff Jenks."

Owen crossed his arms over his chest and glared at him.

Red followed suit.

The deputy huffed a little, shrugged his shoulders, and closed his eye again.

"Fine," he said. "Suit yourselves."

18

Fargo got back to the new room and knocked at the door. He'd made a mistake, not following her out, he supposed. She was probably throwing a fit about that, too.

But nobody answered the door.

In fact, nobody even threw anything breakable at it from the other side—a contingency for which he was prepared.

He tried knocking again, and softly said, "Marga? Honey?"

Nothing.

Maybe she'd done something stupid. Maybe she'd just taken off.

But he'd been sitting down in the restaurant! He would have seen her pass if she'd gone to the livery.

But not, he reminded himself, if she'd gone the back way, taken the side street.

Wonderful.

His brow furrowed, he took out the spare key and let himself in.

But her belongings were still there. Her silver hairbrush, her comb, and buttonhook still lay beside the chipped china washbowl on the bureau, and her trail-dust-covered blue satchel was at the end of the bed.

He let out a clipped sigh of relief and sat down on

the edge of the bed, dangling his hat between his knees. So she was still here. She wasn't lost or laying dead out there in the desert.

This was a comfort to him, but not all that much. She was likely out back in the hotel's privy, but she'd be coming back. And she'd be pissed off. At him, at everybody. But he'd bear the brunt of it, simply because he was handy.

He supposed that he could go and get Mr. Logan, have him tell her, all over again, what he'd told Fargo earlier that evening. But he didn't figure it would be fair to put Logan through that.

Clive Logan was used to retrieving ladies for Sweeney's pleasure, but he wasn't a terrible man. He was just trying to keep his job—that was all—and he was a little ticked about being put upon in such a manner.

He didn't deserve to take what Fargo knew that Marga could dish out. She was a spoiled and silly child in more ways than he knew how to count. She'd never had to learn to deal with people rejecting her. Nobody ever had turned her down, for anything.

Well, she was going to have to deal with it now. Fargo guessed she didn't have much choice.

But he could make it as painless—on himself, anyway—as possible. Tossing his hat on the bed, he stood up and began going around the room, picking up breakable knickknacks and placing them in the lowest bureau drawer. He had the room halfway cleared of throwable objects when the door creaked open.

He turned around, with his hand on his gun—an old habit—but only Marga stood there, in the doorway. She looked, well, awful. Her face was streaked with tears, she was hunched over, and she clung to the door's latch as if it were the only thing keeping her standing.

He took a step toward her, then stopped, unsure of

what to do. After all, he'd never seen her like this. He doubted that anybody had.

And then, slowly, she looked up at him, the tears still streaming down her lovely cheeks, her violet eyes red from crying.

"Oh, Fargo," she said, half-croaking out the words. "You were right. Diego and Rosa were right. And poor Mr. Ethan Posthelwaite!"

She covered her eyes with her hands. "I—I can't sing."

Across the street from the hotel, Cort Cleveland sat in a rocking chair that had been left out on the walk in front of the furniture store. It was also the undertaker's establishment, the irony of which was not lost on Cleveland.

He rocked slowly, there in the dark, studying the hotel, watching lights being lit in one room or another, and wondering which one was Marga's. And if Fargo was in there with her.

The son of a bitch probably was.

Cleveland realized that he was gripping the arms of the rocker nearly hard enough to splinter them, and he made himself let go of them and relax. Well, he tried to, anyway. It was just that the thought of Marga with that tramp, that . . . saddle tramp!

It was too much.

It was why he hadn't fled the city the moment he realized that something had gone very wrong with Owen and Red. It was why he was sitting out here, alone, in the Arizona night.

It was why he was considering throwing the last vestiges of his caution to the wind and barging into their room, shooting.

Oh, he was aware that there would be repercussions.

He'd most likely be arrested. That was the first

thing. The second—and more important—was that he'd most likely be hanged, even if Fargo was nothing but a wretched, west-of-the-Mississippi Natty Bumpo and a credit to no one in particular.

So he knew he couldn't go in there—what was the phrase? Oh, yes. *Guns blazing*—that's what they always said in the half-dime books.

For a moment, he had a brief vision of himself on the cover of one, and barked out an unconscious laugh. Ridiculous!

He then thought that perhaps, if he could ascertain where Fargo was headed next, he could lie in wait for him, on the trail, and ambush him. Lord knows, he'd need the element of surprise.

But then, what if Fargo wasn't the man he wanted at all? Fargo had pushed him out of the picture, certainly, but perhaps this Logan that Marga had spoken about had moved in and displaced Fargo.

He'd been so busy thinking about the immense satisfaction of watching Fargo tumble to the ground—dead and punished and out of the picture—that he hadn't given any thought whatsoever to this other, and very strong, possibility.

Sighing, he reached into his pocket and brought out his next-to-the-last cigar. He lit it, cupping his hands around the lucifer as he puffed, and then tossed the match out into the street.

He was getting sloppy—that was what. He knew it, and he also knew the reason for it—for his muddled thinking, and for the fact that he was sitting out there, contemplating cold-blooded murder in front of who knew how many witnesses—was Marga.

He sighed.

Mr. Clive Logan, then. Or Fargo. Perhaps both of them! He wouldn't put it past Marga.

He leaned back and began to rock. This would take further thought.

He took a puff, and in the night, his cigar glowed red.

Owen, being certain that the deputy was sound asleep, had stealthily—well, as stealthily as was possible for Owen—pulled off his boot and retrieved a small iron pin from his sock.

He'd kept it on his person constantly since he'd escaped from jail that first time. He'd found it in his cell by accident. He still had no idea what that damned thing had been used for in the first place. It was just a stick of iron thicker than a nail and about three inches long—just the right size to wiggle and coax the lock of a cell door open.

Which was what he was attempting to do right now.

Red was no help. He sat on his cot, watching with his mouth open. Owen half expected him to drool.

But he was having trouble. He'd tried twisting and turning his iron pin every which way, and still no luck. Of course, it had never occurred to him to actually take a lock apart and see how it was put together. Or to visit a locksmith's shop. Or to read a book about locks.

He just figured you shoved the pin in the hole and luck took care of the rest.

So far, it wasn't his lucky day.

The deputy shifted in his sleep, agitating his snores. Red sucked in his breath, and Owen pulled the "key" from the lock, freezing until the deputy's breathing settled back into a steady rhythm.

Throwing an unnecessary "Sh!" at Red, Owen went back to work. This time—miracle of miracles—he hit the jackpot. He heard the tumblers turn over, and the door creaked open under his hand.

An elated Red started to say something, then slapped a hand over his own mouth.

Owen, still bootless, crept from the cell and eased

his pistol down from the rack on the wall. And he tiptoed around the desk, behind the deputy, and brought down the grip on that gun as hard as he could.

The deputy slumped to the floor, never having woken.

"Get out here," Owen whispered, and Red obeyed. "Help me drag him in that cell."

Once the deputy was locked safely—if none too gently—away, Owen put his sock back on again, slid his little iron lucky piece home inside it, and then slipped on his boot.

He was glad to do it. The smell was even getting to him.

Red strapped on his gun and Owen strapped on his, and then they both crept carefully out the back door. No one saw them. It was dark outside, but Owen knew where the hotel was, all right. With Red bringing up the rear, he made a beeline for it.

He'd let Red take care of Fargo, and then he, himself, might have a few words with that nosy hotel clerk who'd sent for the sheriff.

Fargo went to the sobbing Marga and gathered her into his arms. She promptly collapsed against his chest, and her sobs became a deluge of tears.

As he whispered, "There, there, it'll be all right, honey," and, "That's it, cry it out," he slowly backed them up toward the bed, then sat down, bringing her with him. And privately he was thinking that this was sure a tough way to learn about the world, but it was about time that she did.

He stroked her hair, kissed her temple, and murmured, "It's all right, baby, it's okay."

She lifted her head. Her eyes were puffy and her face was red, but even with all that, she was still beautiful.

She managed to get out, "It's not fair, Fargo. It's not fair!"

"Life isn't," he said soothingly.

"He let me sing for him," she sniffed. "Mr. Logan. He let me sing. And he stopped me. And he actually held his ears. And he said that whoever told me I could sing needed an ear t-t-trumpet!" She collapsed once again into long, deep sobs and buried her head against Fargo's shoulder.

Fargo bit his lips to keep from smiling. He could imagine how taken Clive Logan must have been with Marga there in the flesh, so to speak. If Logan had said that much to Marga, Fargo knew that his professional opinion must have been ten times worse.

Poor Logan.

Poor Marga.

Poor me! he thought.

"Marga?" he said softly. "Honey?" He tilted her chin up until she was looking into his eyes. God, she looked so . . . bruised. Spiritually, that is.

He went on, "Tomorrow, we'll start back to Quake, all right?"

But she shook her head *no,* and burst into a new round of tears. Fargo rolled his eyes, although he never lessened his hug. He kissed the top of her head again, then said, "I've got to slip outside for a minute, Marga. Will you be okay?"

She nodded without looking up at him. "All right, then. I'll be back."

He let go and rose, and she collapsed back on the bed, weeping, her arm flung over her eyes as she sobbed. And he felt bad about deserting her just when she most needed him.

But if the truth were told, he had to get away from her for a few minutes, or he was afraid he'd laugh in her face.

He had no wish to be cruel. It was just that after putting up with so much horse hockey from her, it was kind of . . . gratifying to see her in such a state.

Hell, she probably needed some time alone, anyway,

he told himself. Just to sort things out. Probably do her good.

And so he let himself out the door, leaned against the hall wall, smiling big enough to almost split his face, then started down the stairs, chuckling.

And he was thinking, *God bless you, Clive Logan, employee of the great entrepreneur Carlos Sweeney, for being an honest man.*

He stepped down into the lobby, chuckling.

19

Cort Cleveland leapt halfway out of his rocking chair, only to be yanked back by Owen's restraining hand clasped firmly across his mouth.

"Shut up!" Owen hissed.

"Mrph mrph," Cort complained beneath Owen's grimy hand.

"Aw, jes' kill him," Red whispered.

Owen let go of Cleveland's mouth. "Kill me? Why kill me?" Cleveland demanded in a whisper. "Your horses are out back of the hotel. I did what you asked! And God only knows were the two of you have been!"

"Jail," Owen said simply.

"The hoosegow!" Red repeated, but with a little more pride. "Owen got us out, yes, he did!"

"Jail?" said Cort, and gulped. He wondered if they'd had to kill anybody to get out of there, but then made himself not think about it.

The less he knew about certain things, he always said, the better.

"There weren't nobody there," added Red.

"In the jail?" asked Cort, one brow cocked.

"No, up to the hotel," explained Red, as if he were speaking to an idiot.

Now, that's the pot calling the kettle black one too

many goddamn times, isn't it? Cleveland thought. But he said nothing.

"Stand up," Owen ordered.

Cleveland did.

"Now, go across to the hotel," said Owen, "and ask which room Fargo's in. Then you go out to the back door—we'll be waitin'—and tell us. Think you can handle that?"

As far as Cleveland was concerned, he wasn't the one who should be asked about "handling" things. He wasn't the one who'd loused things up. Owen and Red had been taking care of that department just fine.

But still, he didn't say a blessed thing except, "Certainly." And smile.

He didn't quite understand why they couldn't ask which room their target was in, but then, so long as they got their task accomplished, it was really none of his business. So he started across the street.

From the corner of his eye, he saw Owen and Red surreptitiously cross the street far to his right.

In *jail*?

Fargo was leaning against the desk, jawing with Archie, when who in the world but Cort Cleveland should walk in the front door!

Fargo cocked his head, and Cleveland stopped stock-still and blinked as if he couldn't believe his eyes. "F-Fargo?" he stuttered.

"Another friend of yours?" Archie moaned, shaking his head. "This is gonna be damned expensive, I can just tell it."

"What do you want, Cleveland?" Fargo asked. He hadn't changed his stance one iota, mainly because he figured Cleveland to be too much of a coward to actually draw down on him.

But still, he was alert. You never could tell about some people.

"I-I-I . . ." Cleveland stuttered, "I guess I'll find

154

someplace else to stay." He backed out the door, the frame of which his frozen hands had been holding open.

The door swung shut behind him, leaving Fargo and the clerk just standing there.

"You got yourself some curious acquaintances, there, Fargo," Archie said.

"Yup," Fargo replied.

"But at least he didn't shoot anything up."

Fargo frowned. "That remains to be seen."

Damn it! Damn it to hell and back again! Cleveland thought as he raced around the hotel and past Owen's and Red's tethered horses to the back alley.

Unaccustomed as he was to running, once he got to Owen and Red, he had to stop and bend over, his hands gripping his thighs for dear life while he tried to catch his breath.

"Well?" Owen asked nastily.

"Yeah!" added an anxious Red. "How 'bout it? My trigger finger's itchin' somethin' fierce!"

Cleveland still didn't have his breath back, but he jabbed a thumb back behind him. "Lobby," he managed to get out. "Fargo. Lobby."

A smile spread over Owen's lips. "That right?" he asked. "Be like shootin' a fox in a trap."

Owen reached behind him and pulled another gun. "That damn deputy's," he said. "Took it for good measure." His smile turned nasty. "Here," he said, handing it to Cleveland.

Cleveland, still panting, took it gingerly. "What? What do you want . . . me to do with this?" he asked between labored breaths.

"I want you should go in the back hall, there," Owen said, pointing to the hotel's back door. "If he tries to get out the back way, don't ask no questions. Just shoot the son of a bitch."

Red cackled. "Shoot him dead!" he added gleefully.

"But you likely ain't gonna have to. I never misses. Never. Do I, Owen?"

Owen rolled his eyes. "There'll be plenty of time to brag you up later, Red. Right now, we gotta get round there before Fargo takes off."

Cleveland, still awkwardly holding the spare gun, nodded dumbly. Panting, though a little less now, he watched Owen and Red round the corner of the hotel, as they headed for the front door.

Owen and Red stood outside the door, their backs plastered to the roughsawn wood, their guns drawn.

"You go in first," Owen whispered.

"You bet," Red answered with a smile.

"On three?" Owen asked.

"Three what?" Red asked, screwing up his face.

Owen sighed. "Just go!"

Red did. He burst through the hotel door and shot the clerk square in the shoulder.

Behind Red, Owen thundered, "Where's Fargo?" even as the clerk was slowly slithering to the ground.

But the clerk didn't answer. He was out cold.

"Jesus Christ!" Owen shouted. "Can't nobody do anything right?"

Red opened his mouth to say something, but was cut off by a gun blast from the alley.

"Cleveland!" Owen shouted. "I'll be damned. Cleveland got him!" And he pushed past Red and headed down the hall, through all the doors, past the bathing room, and out the back door.

Where Fargo stood, leaning up against the opposite building.

"Howdy, Owen," he said. His gun was drawn and pointed directly at Owen's heart.

"Shit!" Owen spat. But his gun was still drawn, too, and he foolishly tried to get off a shot.

Fargo fired first, though. Owen's shot sang off the metal strapping on a nearby barrel, severing it, and

Owen dropped face first into the dirt at the same time the staves of the barrel fell apart and clattered to the ground.

Owen, who had lost his gun and was severely wounded, wasn't out yet, though. He rasped, "Get him, Red! Get the son of a bitch who killed me!"

Owen couldn't exactly see him, but he heard Red ask, "How can you be dead and still be talkin', Owen?"

Owen ground his teeth. "Just shoot him!" he croaked.

Damn, but his chest hurt!

He heard a shot ring out, and then another, right on top of it, and Fargo was still standing there. "Again, dammit!" he tried to shout, but it came out as a whisper. And then Red crumpled on top of him.

"Goddammit, Red," Owen breathed. "You never miss!"

But Red didn't answer. He stared with unseeing eyes, just past Owen's shoulder.

"Goddamn turd bucket," Owen muttered. His chest was really paining him now. He wondered if he was going to die, like Red. And then he wondered what had become of that flimflammer, Cleveland.

"If you're wondering what happened to Cleveland," Fargo said, as if he could read minds, too, "I imagine he's halfway out of town by now. Told him he could take your horse, Owen. Didn't think you'd mind."

Fargo walked near and kicked Owen's gun and Red's even farther away. As if Red could have stretched out and reached it. Hell, he was probably shot through the heart and going home to Jesus directly!

"Hurts," Owen managed to get out.

"Imagine it does," Fargo said. He rolled Red's body away, knelt down and put his hand over the corpse's heart. "Yup, dead," he said.

And then he pulled a short piece of rope out of

his back pocket and proceeded to bind Owen's hands behind him.

"Careful, you bastard!" Owen wheezed, tears of pain brimming over his eyelids.

"Just want you to hold still until the law can pick you up," Fargo said. "Suppose that slug you boys fired in there went directly into the desk clerk?"

With some pride, Owen said, "It did."

"Well, you'd best hope he isn't dead. 'Course, you might hang anyway. I hear they've got a real tough judge in these parts."

"Great," Owen muttered. "Just great."

Fargo got Archie up to the doc's before he strolled up to the jail to report with had happened. He took his time, too.

When he arrived there, he unlocked the cell and let the deputy out—after slopping a bucket of water over him to wake him up. Mad as a sackful of very wet tomcats, the deputy, along with Fargo, went down to the hotel to collect Owen. For Red, they woke up the undertaker.

Fargo didn't mention Cort Cleveland. He figured he understood what drove the man, and he couldn't rightly blame him. He did mention, however, that he'd taken it upon himself to give Owen's horse to a passing stranger who looked down on his luck. The deputy said, "Good riddance. Save the town havin' to board it."

They stripped Owen almost to the skin once they got him to jail, and Fargo discovered the iron pin in his boot.

"Well now, that explains a helluva lot, Mr. Thurst," the deputy said snidely. "Guess that this time, you'll be stayin' with us long enough to meet Judge Claiborne."

"Get me a doctor," replied Owen. "I'm dyin'."

"You can wait," the deputy said. "Slug ain't done

more than glance off your collarbone, so no more'a that wishful thinkin'."

Fargo snorted. He'd been aiming a little lower, but it would do.

At the hotel, Marga had at last stopped crying. She'd barely heard the first shot, being absorbed in her own misery, but she'd heard the last few. Those were what had stopped her tears.

Afraid to leave her room, she had been sitting there quietly, alert for any other sound.

But none came. And neither did Fargo.

She had begun to wonder if perhaps he'd been the target when the door creaked open.

She leapt to her feet and ran to him. "Fargo, Fargo!" she cried. "I was so worried! I heard gunshots, and—"

He touched her face. So calming, so reassuring. "It's all right, honey. They were shooting at me, but I came out on top. The desk clerk's got a bum shoulder out of it, though."

"Who was it? Why would they shoot at you?"

He sat her back down on the bed and explained it all, from beginning to end.

"Cort came after me?" she asked. "I mean, you? And you didn't turn him in?"

"Yes, he did, and no, I didn't," Fargo answered with a smile.

How brave he was, Marga thought, and how wise. She had never noticed before. She should have. She should have noticed a great many things.

She reached up and stroked his face. "I am sorry, Fargo. I am sorry for so much. I have been a spoiled little girl, paying attention to no one but myself. Forgive me?"

"Yes, Marga," Fargo said kindly.

She felt that she didn't deserve kindness from anyone, least of all him. She had driven her poor sister, and her good brother-in-law, half mad with her singing, and they had been kind enough to let her do it, kind enough to hang all those sound-buffering tapestries and to say it was because they were beautiful, not because they would mask the sound of her terrible voice.

So kind, so very kind. And she had been so unappreciative.

Mr. Clive Logan had made no bones about it whatsoever. And Mr. Logan had nothing to gain by lying to her. He had, in fact, quite a bit to lose.

She had believed his words when she hadn't believed Fargo.

She was ashamed.

"Fargo?" she said.

"What, baby?"

"Will you take me back to Quake now?" She had to apologize to so many people, not the least of which was her voice teacher. Diego Madrid must have paid him a fortune to put up with her!

"Yes, but not now," Fargo said.

She smiled. "In the morning, then?"

He nodded. "In the morning," he murmured, and then he kissed her.

LOOKING FORWARD!

**The following is the opening
section of the next novel in the exciting
Trailsman series from Signet:**

THE TRAILSMAN #269
Devil's Den

*Indian Territory, 1860—
Where evil men brew bad whiskey
and worse trouble.*

Skye Fargo knew he was being followed.

The big man in buckskins didn't turn around in the saddle to study his back trail, but he knew somebody was there. His lake-blue eyes narrowed as he felt the skin crawl in the middle of his back, as if someone were drawing a bead on the spot. He kept the Ovaro moving steadily, varying the pace every now and then just to confirm his suspicions.

Better to draw the follower on for a spell, he thought. Bide his time and wait for the right moment to turn the tables on whoever it was. Assuming, of course, that nobody bushwhacked him first.

Whoever was back there, they sure as hell knew how to spoil a beautiful day, Fargo told himself.

If there was one thing the Trailsman appreciated— besides a pretty woman, an honest poker game, and a glass of good whiskey, that is—it was nice weather. He had spent most of his life dealing with extreme heat and cold, drought and flood, sandstorms and snowstorms. A day such as today, with clear blue skies, warm sunshine, and a cool breeze, was something to be savored.

He had followed the Arkansas River westward toward Fort Smith for several days and expected to reach the town before night fell again. Mountains rose to the north and south of the river valley, some of them rounded and covered with trees, others rockier and rising to craggy peaks. Spring was far enough along so that wildflowers bloomed in some of the meadows, perfuming the air with their scent. Fargo was the sort of man who could find beauty in nature no matter where he was, but a fella didn't have to look very hard for it around here.

Too bad a serpent had made its way into this Eden. Fargo figured the man trailing him was up to no good. Otherwise he would have announced himself before now.

Still following the river, Fargo rode around a sharp bend in the stream, past a large boulder. This was the spot, he sensed immediately. He sent the big black-and-white stallion off the road and into the trees that covered the hillside on his left.

Fargo swung down from the saddle and led the Ovaro deeper into the woods. He tied the reins around the trunk of a tree and then hurried back toward the river and the boulder that loomed next to the road. Fargo climbed part of the way up the rugged chunk of rock and crouched there, out of sight of the trail.

He waited with the innate patience of a born frontiersman until he heard the steady beat of a horse's hooves on the road. The animal and its rider drew even with the boulder and started past it. Fargo scrambled the rest of the way to the top and found himself looking down on the rider's broad-brimmed black hat. He dived off the boulder in a flying tackle.

His arms went around the man on horseback and tore him out of the saddle. With a wild, startled cry, the man fell, landing hard on the ground with Fargo on top of him. The impact knocked the breath out of the man. He lay there gasping for air as Fargo rolled to the side and came up drawing his Colt.

Fargo didn't know the man, though there was something vaguely familiar about him. He was burly and mostly bald, with a fringe of dark hair around his naked scalp and bushy muttonchop whiskers on his face. His rough clothing showed a lot of wear. He had an old pistol tucked behind his belt.

The man started to push himself upright, but the sight of Fargo's Colt trained on him made him freeze. "Just rest easy, friend," Fargo said in a flinty voice that wasn't friendly at all. "Who are you, and why have you been following me?"

A sullen look came over the man's face as he propped himself on an elbow and rubbed his jaw. "Are you crazy, mister?" he whined. "I don't know you. Why'd you jump me?"

"You've been riding behind me all afternoon."

"Well, hell, is it a crime for a fella to ride along a road? That's what it's there for!"

"You slowed down every time I slowed down," Fargo pointed out, "and you rode faster every time I did. But you always stayed just far enough back so that if I turned around you could duck into the trees and not be spotted. That's what you thought, anyway."

"I don't know what the hell you're talkin'—" The man stopped short, and Fargo saw the determination to continue the argument go out of him. "I told Barker it was a mistake. You can't go followin' the damned Trailsman without him catchin' on."

Fargo gestured with the barrel of the Colt. "Get up, and tell me who Barker is. Did the two of you plan to rob me?"

The man climbed laboriously to his feet. He still seemed to be a little shaky from being knocked off his horse. He passed a hand across his eyes and swayed slightly. "Barker's just a fella I met a few days ago in Dardenelle. Don't know why he wanted to follow you. He never did say."

Dardenelle was a settlement to the east, also on the Arkansas River. Fargo had stayed at a hotel there the previous night. He wasn't surprised that was where the mysterious Barker and this man, name still unknown, had spotted him. He hadn't made any secret of his presence. He'd eaten supper in the hotel dining room and had a few drinks in a tavern just down the street.

Fargo was on his way to Fort Smith in response to a message from an old friend. He wondered if his two followers had any connection with that situation.

And for that matter, where in blazes was Barker, anyway?

The man he had captured let out a groan and put both hands on his head. "I don't feel so good, Fargo," he complained. "I hit my head when you knocked me off my horse. Feels like I might've busted something. Ohhhhh . . ."

He staggered to the side, and as he did so, his right

hand dropped from his head toward his waist. Fargo's keen eyes saw the move and recognized it for what it was—a trick. The man's hand closed around the butt of his pistol and jerked it from behind his belt.

Fargo fired first, but the man wasn't acting like he was injured now. Instead, he threw himself to the side with surprising speed, so that Fargo's slug went harmlessly past him. The gun in his hand roared, sending a bullet sizzling by Fargo's ear.

Before Fargo could squeeze off a second shot, another gun blasted somewhere nearby. That would be Barker, Fargo thought as something tugged at the sleeve of his buckskin shirt. He flung himself backward, diving to the ground and rolling into the shelter of the big rock from which he had tackled the bald man.

A bullet smacked into the rock and sent dust and stone shards showering down around Fargo. He spotted the bald man hurrying toward some trees on the riverbank and triggered a fast shot. It clipped the bald man's leg and sent him tumbling off his feet with a pained yelp.

Hoofbeats sounded from the road, back to the east. Fargo had the boulder between him and whoever was coming, probably Barker. He waited, the Colt ready in his hand, but then the hoofbeats stopped abruptly. When they resumed a few seconds later, they were going the other direction.

Barker must have changed his mind about continuing the attack. He was taking off for the tall and uncut instead.

That left the bald man, who was wounded but still dangerous. Fargo came up in a crouch, burst out from behind the rock, and ran across the road. No more shots sounded as he threw himself down in the grass. He lay there listening intently as his heart hammered in his chest.

He heard the sound of the river rushing over its rocky streambed. Earlier, birds had been singing in the trees, but they were all gone now, frightened off by the shots. Fargo listened harder.

A rustling in the grass, like a snake.

But it was too early in the season for snakes to be crawling.

Suddenly, with a furious shout, the bald man heaved up out of the grass and lunged toward Fargo. The gun in his hand roared as flame geysered from its barrel. Fargo rolled onto his back and felt the ground shiver under him as a bullet slammed into the dirt less than a foot away. The Colt bucked against his palm as he fired.

The bald man went backward as if somebody had just slammed a tree trunk across his face. Fargo saw the pistol fly through the air as the man dropped it. With a lithe motion, the Trailsman uncoiled from the ground and stalked forward, keeping his revolver trained on the fallen man.

The front of the rough linsey-woolsey shirt under the black vest was stained with blood. The man coughed as he lay on his back, and more blood welled from his mouth. He looked up at Fargo from hate-filled eyes in which the life was fading fast.

"You . . . bastard," the dying man grated. "Told Barker . . . not to . . . come after . . ."

He couldn't finish. His final breath rattled in his throat. The muscles in his arms and legs spasmed for a few seconds, and then he was motionless in death.

Fargo looked up and down the river, checking for any signs of the other man, but no one was in sight. Barker, whoever he was, was gone.

Fargo's hat had fallen off when he leaped from the boulder. Now, the cool breeze he had enjoyed so much earlier riffled his thick black hair, but it wasn't the same.

No, sir, he thought, this beautiful day just wasn't anywhere near as nice anymore. Not after two men had tried to kill him and he didn't have the slightest idea why.

Fargo caught the dead man's horse, hefted the corpse over the saddle, and lashed it down. Then he fetched the Ovaro from the hiding place in the trees and resumed his journey to Fort Smith, leading the other mount with its grisly burden. Maybe somebody at Fort Smith would recognize the dead man.